Go ahead and scream.

No one can hear you. You're no longer in the safe world you know.

You've taken a terrifying step . . .

into the darkest corners of your imagination.

You've opened the door to . . .

the NiGHTMARE room

Dear Diary, I'm Dead

R.L. STINE

AVON BOOKS

An Imprint of HarperCollinsPublishers

PARACHUTE PRESS

Dear Diary, I'm Dead

For information address:
HarperCollins Children's Books,
a division of HarperCollins Publishers,
1350 Avenue of the Americas,
New York, NY 10019.

Library of Congress Catalog Card Number: 00-106530
ISBN 0-06-440903-1

First Avon edition, 2000

Visit us on the World Wide Web!
www.harperchildrens.com

Welcome...

Hello, I'm R.L. Stine. Do you ever wish you could see into the future? Would it make you happy to know what questions are on tomorrow's history test? Or which team is going to win the basketball game Friday night?

Knowing the future made Alex Smith very happy. You see, Alex has a bad habit. He likes to make bets with his friends.

One day, Alex finds a very special diary. The diary tells Alex the future—all he needs to know to win every bet.

Alex thinks he's lucky.

But sometimes it doesn't help to know the future. Sometimes the future holds some terrifying surprises. You see, when Alex opened the cover to the diary, he opened the door . . . to THE NIGHTMARE ROOM.

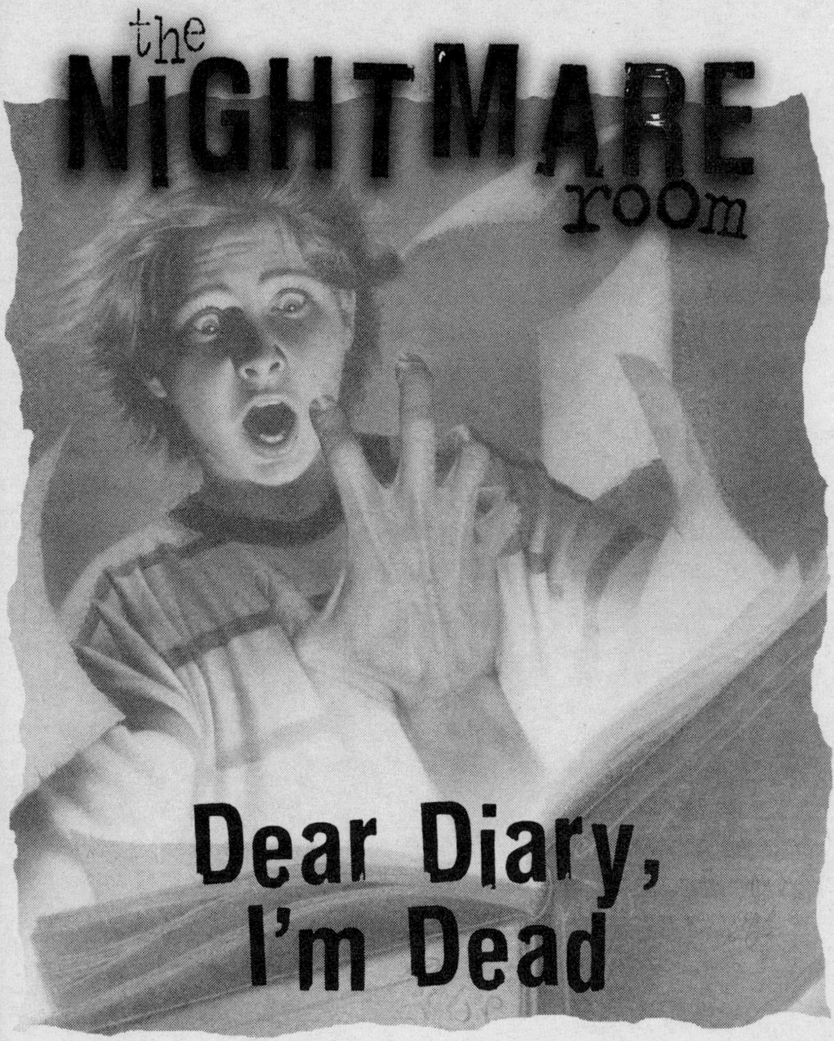
the NIGHTMARE room
Dear Diary,
I'm Dead

DEAR DIARY,

My hands are shaking so badly, I don't know if I can write in you today. I was so scared last night. I'm still trembling.

Maybe I should start at the beginning. You know my friends Chip and Shawn and I have been talking about camping out in Full Moon Woods for nearly a year. Well, last night we finally did it.

What a mistake!

We thought it was going to be cool. We loaded all our gear into my dad's van, and he dropped us off at the dirt path that leads into the woods.

"Stick to the path, Alex," Dad called. "It will lead you to the creek. I'll pick you up right here tomorrow morning." The tires spun in the dirt as he drove away.

It was a cloudy afternoon. As soon as we stepped into the woods, it grew even darker. Our backpacks were bulging. And the canvas tent weighed a ton.

But we didn't mind. We were finally on our own in the woods. We walked quickly, following the path, making our way toward the creek.

Shawn started to sing an old Beatles song. Chip and I joined in. I loved the way our voices echoed off the trees.

"We should have brought our guitars," I said. All three of us play guitar, and we're starting a band.

Chip laughed. "Great idea, Alex. Where would we plug them in?"

"We'd need a very long extension cord!" I replied.

We were laughing and singing, enjoying the fresh cool air and the crunch of our shoes over the carpet of fat brown leaves.

The path ended, but we kept walking. I was pretty sure the creek was straight ahead. It grew even darker, and a cold wind swirled around us.

We walked for at least an hour before we realized we were totally lost.

"We should be able to hear the creek," Shawn said. He set down his backpack and stretched. "Where is it? Did we go in the right direction?"

"We'll never find it now," Chip sighed. "It's too dark."

A gust of wind sent dead leaves flying all around us. "Are there bears in these woods?" Shawn asked. He sounded a little frightened.

"No. But there are bunny rabbits that can chew you to bits!" I joked.

Chip laughed but Shawn didn't. I shivered and wrapped my yellow windbreaker tighter around me.

"Which way is the path?" Shawn asked, turning back. He pointed. "Is that the way we came? Maybe we should go back that way."

A hooting sound made me jump. A bird on a low tree branch. It hooted again, peering down at us.

"I don't want to go back," I said. "Let's keep going. The creek is this way. I know it."

But Shawn and Chip wanted to stay right there and pitch the tent. It wasn't a bad place. A circle of tall grass surrounded by tall trees. So I agreed.

We tossed our backpacks in a pile and started to unroll the tent.

That's when I had the feeling for the first time—the feeling that we were being watched.

I felt a prickling on the back of my neck. I heard a snapping sound behind us, like someone stepping on dry twigs.

I spun around. But I didn't see anyone. The trees tilted toward each other, as if closing in on us.

"What's your problem?" Shawn asked. "Did you see an animal?"

I laughed. "Yeah. A herd of buffalo."

We struggled with the tent. The gusting wind kept blowing it out of our hands. We finally got it to stand. But then the wind kept blowing out our campfire.

By the time we finished dinner, it was late. All three of us were yawning. My shoulders ached from carrying the heavy backpack.

We decided to climb into the tent and go to sleep. Shawn and Chip crawled inside. I started to follow them—then stopped.

I had the strange feeling again. The prickling on the back of my neck. Who was watching us?

I squinted through the misty darkness. I sucked in my breath when I saw dull gray circles—several pairs of them—floating low between the trees.

Eyes?

I dove into the tent. We slept in our clothes under wool blankets. The wool felt scratchy. The tent was damp from dew.

We couldn't sleep. We started to tell each other jokes. We were kidding around and laughing a lot.

But we stopped laughing when the howls started.

They were low at first, like ambulance sirens far in the distance. But then they sounded closer, louder. And we knew they were animal howls.

"I . . . hope it's dogs!" Shawn exclaimed. "Maybe it's just some wild dogs."

We huddled close together. We all knew we weren't hearing dogs. We were hearing wolf howls.

So close. . . . So close we could hear the harsh, shallow breaths between the howls.

And then the soft crunch of footsteps outside the tent.

They were here! The howling creatures! The tent flap blew open.

My friends and I let out screams.

Two men in black leather jackets leaned down to peer into our tent. One of them raised a flashlight. He moved the light slowly from face to face. "Are you kids okay?" he asked.

"Wh-who are you?" I asked.

"Forest Patrol," the other man said.

"Yeah. Right. Forest Patrol," his partner repeated.

They both stared at us so hard. Their eyes were cold, not friendly at all.

"The woods really aren't safe," the man with the flashlight said. "Not safe at all."

His partner nodded. "First thing in the morning, you should get yourselves to the road. It's right up there." He pointed.

We promised we would. We thanked them for checking on us.

But I didn't like the way they stared. They didn't look like forest rangers. And as soon as they left, the frightening howls started up again. Howls all around us.

We didn't sleep at all that night. We lay awake, staring up at the tent walls, listening to the animal howls.

The next morning, as soon as sunlight began trickling down through the trees, we jumped up. We hurried out of the tent and began to pack.

I started to fold up the tent—but stopped when I saw something strange on the ground. "Hey—!" I called out to Chip and Shawn. "Look!"

I pointed to the footprints in the soft dirt. Two pairs that led from the woods to the front of our tent.

The Forest Rangers' prints.

All three of us stared, stared in shock and horror.

Their prints weren't human. They were animal paws.

Animal paws in the dirt.

Wolf prints!

"Alex, is any of that true?" Miss Gold asked.

I rolled the pages of my story between my hands. "No," I told her. "I made it all up."

"You and Chip and Shawn never went camping?" she asked, peering at me over the rims of her glasses.

"No. Never," I said.

"He's afraid of poison ivy!" Chip called out.

The whole class laughed.

"He's afraid of *trees!*" another kid chimed in.

The whole class laughed even harder.

"He's afraid of bugs!" Shawn added.

No one laughed at that. No one ever laughs at Shawn's jokes. He's a good guy, but he just isn't funny.

"Well, that is an excellent short story," Miss Gold said. "One of the best we've heard this week. Thank you for sharing it with the class, Alex. Very good work."

She waved me back to my seat. But I didn't move

from the front of the classroom. "Aren't you going to tell me my grade?" I crossed my fingers behind my back.

"Oh. Right." Miss Gold pushed the glasses up on her nose. "I'll give you a B-plus."

"Huh?" I let out a groan. "Not an A?"

"B-plus," she repeated.

"But—why?" I demanded.

She brushed her blond hair off her forehead. "Well . . . you did very well with the plot. But I think you need to work on describing your characters better. We don't really know what Chip and Shawn look like—do we?"

"But they're sitting right there!" I protested, pointing at my two friends. "You *know* what they look like!"

"Real ugly!" a kid shouted from the back of the room.

Big laughter.

But I wasn't laughing. I needed an A.

"You need to describe them in the story," Miss Gold continued. "And we don't know what's different about them. You didn't give them real personalities."

"But—" I started.

"And I think you need more description of the woods," she said. "More detail. You know, Alex, the more little details you add to a story, the more *real* it becomes."

Tessa Wayne was waving her hand frantically in

8

the air. "There's something I don't understand," she said. "If the two men were wolves, where did they get the leather jackets? I mean, they were completely dressed, right? But they're wolves? And how did they get the flashlight?"

"Good questions, Tessa," Miss Gold said.

I rolled my eyes. Tessa always asks the good questions. That's why I hate her guts.

"The men were werewolves," I explained, sighing. "Not regular wolves."

"Well, the bell is about to ring," Miss Gold said, gazing up at the wall clock. She turned back to me. "I just had an idea. You did such a good job with the diary format. I mean, writing your story as a diary entry was very clever."

"Thanks," I said weakly. So why didn't she give me an A?

"You should keep a *real* diary, Alex," she continued. "Write in it every day. You can hand it in at the end of the year for extra credit."

"Really?" I said. "Okay. Thanks."

I saw Tessa's hand fly up. I knew what she was going to say.

"Miss Gold, I want to start a diary too. Can I do a diary for extra credit?"

"Yes," Miss Gold replied. "Anyone in class can keep a diary. Very good idea."

The bell rang.

I hurried to my seat and started to shove my story

into my backpack. I felt a sharp tap on my back. I knew who it was.

"Pay up, Alex," Tessa said. She stuck her hand in front of my face.

"Excuse me?" I tried to play innocent.

"Pay up," she insisted. "You bet me five dollars you'd get an A on that story. You lost."

"A B-plus is almost an A," I said.

She waved the hand in my face. "Pay up."

I reached into my jeans pocket. "But . . . I only have *three* dollars," I said.

"Then why did you bet me?" Tessa demanded. "You know you never win a bet against me. You always lose."

"Wait a sec," I said. I caught up with Chip and Shawn at the door. "Pay up," I said, blocking their way.

They both groaned. Then they reached into their pockets, and each of them handed me a dollar bill.

I hurried back to Tessa. "Okay, I've got the five," I said. I handed it to her.

"What was *that* about?" she asked, motioning toward Chip and Shawn.

"I bet them each a dollar that after you heard my story, you'd want to write in a diary too."

Tessa blushed. Her cheeks turned an angry red. "Big deal," she muttered. "So you won two bucks from your friends. But you're such a loser, Alex. Now you're totally broke—right?"

I pulled out my pockets. Empty. "Yeah. I'm broke."

Tessa grinned. "I love making bets with you," she said. She held the money up in front of my face and counted the five dollars one by one. "It's like taking candy from a baby."

"Wait a minute—" I told her.

An idea had flashed into my mind. An awesome idea. An idea that would turn me from a loser into a winner.

"I want to make one more bet with you," I told Tessa. "A really big bet."

"You did *what?*" Shawn screamed. "Alex, are you totally whacked?"

"I'm going to win this one," I said.

"But you *never* win a bet with Tessa," Chip said. "How could you bet a hundred dollars?"

We were in Chip's garage after school, tuning up our guitars. The garage had only one electrical outlet, so we could plug in only two amps. That meant that one of us had to play acoustic, even though we all had electric guitars.

"I won't need a hundred dollars," I said, "because I'm going to win."

Sproinnnng.

I broke a string. I let out a groan. "I'll just play without it," I muttered.

Shawn shook his head. "You're crazy, Alex. After what happened with McArthur and the flag . . ."

"That was a sure thing!" I cried. "I should have won that bet!"

Just thinking about it made me angry.

A few weeks ago, I made a deal with Mr. McArthur. He's one of the janitors at school. Except he's not called a janitor. He's called a maintenance engineer.

McArthur is a nice guy. He and I kid around sometimes. So I made a deal with him.

He raises the flag every morning on the flagpole in front of our school. So I paid him five dollars to raise it upside down on Wednesday morning.

Then I dragged Tessa to school early and bet her ten dollars that he would raise the flag upside down.

"You're crazy, Alex," Tessa said, rolling her eyes. "McArthur has never slipped up like that."

He will *this* morning, I thought happily. I started planning how I'd spend Tessa's ten bucks.

How was I to know that Mrs. Juarez, the principal, would arrive at school just when McArthur was raising the flag?

She came walking up the steps and saw McArthur. So she stopped in front of the pole, raised her hand to her heart, and waited to watch the flag go up.

Of course McArthur chickened out. He raised the flag right side up.

I didn't blame him. What could he do with her standing right there?

But I had to pay Tessa the ten bucks. And then McArthur said he'd pay me back my five dollars in a week or so. Not a good day.

"It's my turn," I told my two friends. "Tessa has won about three hundred bets in a row. So it's definitely my turn!"

"But why did you bet her that your diary would be more exciting than hers?" Shawn asked.

"Because it will be," I said. "Tessa is real smart and gets perfect grades. That's because all she does is study. She spends all her time on homework and projects for extra credit. She's so totally boring! So her diary can't be exciting. No way!"

"Who's going to decide whose diary is the best?" Chip asked.

"We're going to let Miss Gold decide," I said. "But it won't be a hard choice for her. This is one bet I'm not going to lose."

"Want to bet?" Chip asked.

I squinted across the garage at him. "Excuse me?"

"Bet you five dollars Tessa wins this bet too."

"You're on!" I said. I slapped him a high-five.

"Count me in," Shawn said. "Five bucks on Tessa."

"You guys are real losers," I groaned. "Let's play. What's the first song?"

"How about 'Purple Haze'?" Chip suggested. "It's our best song."

"It's our *only* song," I muttered.

We counted off, tapping our feet, and started to play "Purple Haze." We played for about ten seconds, when we heard a loud, crackling *pop*.

The music stopped and the lights went out.

We'd blown the fuses again.

A short while later, I dragged my guitar case into the house. Mom greeted me at the door. "I've been waiting for you," she said. "I have a surprise."

I tossed my backpack onto the floor. Then I tossed my jacket on top of it.

"Don't tell me. Let me guess," I said. "I'll bet you five dollars it's a puppy. You finally bought me that puppy I asked for when I was six?"

Mom shook her head. "No puppy. You know your dad is allergic."

"He can breathe at work," I said. "Why does he have to breathe at home?"

Mom laughed. She thinks I'm a riot. She laughs at just about everything I say.

"I'll bet five dollars it's . . . a DVD player!" I exclaimed.

Mom shook her head. "No way, Alex. And stop betting every second. That's such a bad habit. Is that why you're broke all the time?"

I didn't answer that question. "What's the surprise?" I asked.

"Come on. I'll show you." Mom pulled me upstairs to my bedroom. I could see she was excited.

She moved behind me and pushed me into the room. "Check it out, Alex!"

I stared at the big desk against the wall. It was made of dark wood and it had two rows of drawers on the sides.

I stepped up to it. The desktop had a million little scratches and cracks in it.

"It's . . . it's old!" I said.

"Yes, it's an antique," Mom replied. "Your dad and I found it at that little antiques store on Montrose near the library."

I ran my hand over the old wood. Then I sniffed a couple of times. "It's kind of smelly," I murmured.

"It won't be smelly after we polish it up," Mom said. "It will be like new. It's a beautiful old desk. So big and roomy. You'll have space for your computer and your PlayStation, and all your homework supplies."

"I guess," I said.

Mom gave me a playful shove. "Just say 'Thank you, Mom. It's a nice surprise. I really needed a desk like this.'"

"Thank you, Mom," I repeated. "It's a nice surprise. I really needed a desk like this."

She laughed. "Go ahead. Sit down. Try it out." She wheeled a new desk chair over to the desk. It was chrome with red leather.

"What an awesome chair!" I said. "Does it tilt back? Does it go up and down?"

"Yes, it does everything," Mom said. "It's a thrill ride!"

"Cool!" I dropped into the chair and wheeled it up to the old desk.

The phone rang downstairs. Mom hurried to answer it.

I tilted the chair back. Then I leaned forward, smoothing my hands over the desk's dark wood. I wonder who owned it before me, I thought.

I pulled open the top desk drawer. It jammed at first. I had to tug hard to slide it open. The drawer was empty.

I slid open the next drawer. The next. Both empty. The air inside the drawers was kind of sour smelling.

I leaned down and pulled open the bottom drawer.

"Hey—what's that?"

Something hidden at the back of the drawer. A small, square black book.

I reached in and lifted it from the drawer.

Then I blew the thick layer of dust off the cover and raised it close to see what it was.

A diary!

I stared at the dusty book, turning it over in my hands. What a strange coincidence!

I rubbed my hand over the black leather cover. Then I opened the book and flipped quickly through the pages.

They were completely blank.

I'll use this to write my diary for Miss Gold, I decided. I'll write my first entry tonight. And I'll write it in ink. Miss Gold will like that.

I set the diary down on the desk and thought about what I would write.

First, I'll describe my friends, I decided. Miss Gold said I needed more description, more details. I stared at the old diary and planned what I would say.

I'll start with me. How would I describe myself?

Well, I'm tall and kind of wiry. I have wild brown hair that I hate because it won't stay down. My mom says I'm always fidgeting. I can't sit still. My dad says I talk too fast and too much.

What else? Hmmm . . . I'm kind of smart. I like to hang out with my friends and make them laugh. I'm a pretty good guitar player. I'd like to make a lot of money and get really rich because I'm always broke, and I hate it.

That's enough about me. What about Chip? How would I describe Chip?

Well . . . he's short. He's chubby. He has really short brown hair and a round baby face. He looks about six, even though he's twelve like me.

Chip wears baggy clothes. He likes to wrestle around and pretend to fight. He's always in a good mood, always ready to laugh. He's a terrible guitar player, but he thinks he's Jimi Hendrix.

Shawn is very different from Chip. He's very intense, very serious. He worries a lot. He's not a wimp or anything. He just worries.

Shawn has brown eyes, orangy hair that's almost carrot colored, and lots of freckles. He gets better grades in school than Chip and me because he works a lot harder.

Who else should I describe? Do I have to describe Tessa? Yes, I guess I should. She'll probably pop up in the diary from time to time.

I guess Tessa is kind of cute. But she's so stuck-up, who cares?

She has straight blond hair, green eyes, a turned-up nose like an elf nose, and a little red heart-shaped mouth. She's very preppy and perfect-looking.

Yes. That's good. Tessa wants to be perfect all the time. And she hangs out only with girls who are just like her.

I flipped through the empty diary one more time. I'm pretty good at description, I decided. I couldn't wait to write this stuff down.

And what else should I write about? I'll write about how my parents bought me a new desk, and how I found a blank diary in the bottom drawer just when I needed a diary. Very cool!

I leaned back in the new desk chair, very pleased with myself. I tilted the chair back a few times. Then I raised and lowered the seat, just to see how it worked.

I heard Dad come home. Then I heard Mom calling me to dinner. I tucked the diary into the top desk drawer and hurried down to the dining room.

"How's the new desk?" Dad asked.

"Excellent," I told him. "Thanks, Dad."

He passed the bowl of spaghetti. "Did you have band practice this afternoon?"

"Yes, kind of," I replied. "We blew the fuses again. We really need a better place to rehearse."

Mom chuckled. "Your band needs a lot of things. Like a singer, for example. None of you guys can sing a note. And how about someone who *doesn't* play guitar?"

I rolled my eyes. "Thanks for the encouragement, Mom."

Dad laughed too. "What do you call your band? Strings and More Strings?"

"Ha-ha," I said. Dad has such a lame sense of humor. He's not even as funny as Shawn, who is never funny!

"Bet you ten dollars that we get good enough to win the junior high talent contest," I said.

"Alex, no betting," Mom said sternly.

They started talking to each other, and I concentrated on my spaghetti and turkey meatballs. We used to have real meatballs. But Mom became a health freak. And now all of our meat is made out of turkey.

After dinner, I practically flew upstairs to get started on my diary. I found a black marker pen to write with. Then I sat down in the new desk chair and pulled the diary out of the drawer.

I'll start with an introduction about how I found the diary, I decided. Then I'll describe my friends and me.

I opened the diary to the first page. And let out a gasp.

The page had been completely blank when I found the book this afternoon. But now it was covered with writing. There was already a diary entry there!

At the top of the page, a date was written: *Tuesday, January 16*.

"Huh?" I squinted hard at it. Today's date was

21

Monday the fifteenth.

"This is too weird!" I said out loud.

A diary entry for tomorrow?

My eyes ran over the handwritten words. I couldn't focus. I was too surprised and confused.

And then I uttered another gasp when I made another impossible discovery.

The diary entry was written in *my handwriting*!

A diary entry for tomorrow in my handwriting? How can that be? I wondered.

My hands were shaking. So I set the open book down on the desktop. Then I leaned over it and eagerly started to read.

DEAR DIARY,

The diary war has started, and I know I'm going to win. I can't wait to see the look on Tessa's face when she has to hand over one hundred big ones to me.

I ran into Tessa in the hall at school, and I started teasing her about our diaries. I said that she and I should share what we're writing—just for fun. I'll read hers, and she could read mine.

Tessa said no way. She said she doesn't want me stealing her ideas. I said, "Whatever." I was just trying to give her a break and let her see how much better my diary is going to be than hers.

Then I went into geography class, and Mrs. Hoff horrified everyone by giving a surprise test on chapter eight. No one had studied chapter eight. And the test was really hard—two essay questions and twenty multiple choice.

Why does Mrs. Hoff think it's so much fun to surprise us like that?

The diary entry ended there. I stared at the words until they became a blur.

My hands were still shaking. My forehead was chilled by a cold sweat.

My handwriting. And it sounded like the way I wrote.

But how could that be? How did an entry for tomorrow get in there?

I read it again. Then I flipped through the book, turning the pages carefully, scanning each one.

Blank. All blank. The rest of the pages were blank.

I turned back to tomorrow's entry and read it for a third time.

Was it true? It couldn't be—could it?

What if it is? I asked myself. What if Mrs. Hoff *does* spring a surprise test on us? Then, I'd be the only one who knew about it.

I'd be the only one to pass the test.

I closed the diary and shoved it into the desk drawer. Then I found my geography textbook, opened it to chapter eight, and studied it for the next two hours.

The next morning, I ran into Tessa in the hall outside Mrs. Hoff's room. "Nice shirt, Alex," she sneered, turning up her already-turned-up nose. "Did you puke on it this morning, or is that just the color?"

"I borrowed it from *you*—remember?" I shot back. Pretty good reply, huh?

"How is your diary coming?" Tessa asked. "Or do you want to give up and just pay me the hundred dollars now?" She waved to two of her friends across the hall, two girls who look just like her.

"My diary is going to be awesome," I said. "I wrote twelve pages in it last night."

I know, I know. That was a lie. I just wanted to see Tessa react.

She sneered at me. "Twelve pages? You don't know that many words!" She laughed at her own joke.

"I have an idea," I said. "Why don't we share each other's diaries?"

She frowned at me. "Excuse me?"

"I'll read your diary, and you can read mine," I said. "You know. Just for fun."

"Fun?" She made a disgusted face at me, puckering up that tiny heart-shaped mouth. "No way, Alex. I'm not showing you my diary. I don't want you stealing my ideas!"

Oh wow.

Oh wow!

That's just what Tessa said in the diary entry.

Was the diary entry coming true? Was it all really going to happen?

I suddenly felt dizzy, weak. How could a book predict the future?

I shook my head hard, trying to shake the dizziness away.

"Alex? Are you okay?" Tessa asked. "You look so weird all of a sudden. What's wrong with you?"

"Uh . . . nothing," I said. "I'm fine."

The bell was about to ring. I gazed into Mrs. Hoff's classroom. It was filling up with kids.

I turned back to Tessa. "Uh . . . you haven't read chapter eight yet, have you?" I asked.

"No. Not yet," Tessa replied. "Why?"

"No reason," I said, trying to hide my grin.

I followed her into the room. I waved to Chip and Shawn. Then I dropped my backpack to the floor and slid into my seat at the back of the room.

Mrs. Hoff was leaning over her desk, shuffling through a pile of folders. She has straight black hair and flour-white skin, and she always wears black.

Some kids call her Hoff the Goth. But that doesn't make sense, and it doesn't even rhyme.

I sat stiffly in my seat, watching her, tapping my fingers tensely on the desktop. My heart started to race.

Is she going to give the test? I wondered.

Is the rest of the diary entry going to come true?

My heart thudded in my chest. I leaned forward so far, I nearly fell off my seat.

Is she going to announce the test? Is she?

Gripping the desktop with both hands, I held my breath and watched her.

"Let's all settle down now," Mrs. Hoff said, straightening one sleeve of her black sweater. "We are going to have a busy morning."

A busy morning? What did that mean?

A test?

I couldn't hold my breath any longer. I let it out in a long *whoosh*.

"Please clear your desks," Mrs. Hoff said. "Take out paper and pencils, everyone. We're having a surprise test on chapter eight."

"YESSSS!" I cried.

My shout rose up over the groans and moans of all the other kids.

Everyone turned to gape at me.

I could feel my face growing hot. I knew that I was blushing.

Mrs. Hoff tossed back her black hair and snickered. "Since when do you like tests, Alex?"

"I . . . uh . . . didn't hear you right," I answered, thinking fast. "I thought you said we were going to have a *rest!*"

The whole class burst out laughing.

I like making people laugh—but I hate being laughed at. At least it got me off the hook.

Mrs. Hoff handed around the test papers. I checked mine out carefully. Two essay questions and twenty multiple choice.

Yes! Just like in the diary entry.

It was all true. All of it!

The diary predicted the future.

Several times I had to stop myself from humming as I took the test. This was sweet, so sweet! I knew everything! It was going to be my best geography score ever.

I could hear the other kids moaning unhappily. Across the room, Shawn was slapping his forehead, frowning down at his test paper.

I finished ten minutes before the bell rang. The other kids were still writing like crazy, groaning in misery, scratching their heads.

When the bell rang, the room was silent. Kids slowly handed in their test papers. Their faces were green, sick looking.

"I flunked it," Chip sighed out in the hall. "I totally flunked it."

Shawn slumped behind him. "I didn't know enough to flunk it!" he declared.

A pretty good joke for Shawn. Only I don't think he was joking.

"How did you do, Alex?" he asked.

"Not bad," I said. "I might have aced it."

I turned away from their shocked stares to greet Tessa.

She slunk into the hall, defeated, wrung out. Even her hair looked wilted.

"That was rough," she groaned. "Why didn't she tell us to study that chapter?"

I couldn't keep a grin from spreading across my face. "Tessa, bet you five dollars I aced it," I said.

Her mouth dropped open.

"Alex, save your money!" Shawn warned. "That's crazy. You know you never win a bet against Tessa."

"You can't win that bet!" Chip chimed in.

"Five bucks," I repeated, ignoring them. "Want to bet, Tessa?"

She narrowed her eyes at me. She studied me hard. "You want to bet me that you aced that surprise test?"

My grin grew wider. I tried to keep a straight face. But I just couldn't.

"I don't like that grin," Tessa said. "No bet."

"But, Tessa—" I started.

She spun away and trotted around the corner, her blond hair sagging limply behind her.

"Alex, you can't win against her," Shawn said. "Why do you keep trying?"

"Maybe I can win," I told him. "Maybe I'm going to start winning big-time."

"Are we going to practice after school?" Chip asked. "I found a better extension cord for the garage. Maybe it won't blow the fuses."

"We need to learn some new songs," Shawn said. "I downloaded the chords for 'Stairway to Heaven.'"

"Cool," Chip said. He began strumming his stomach, humming the melody, doing a loud air-guitar version of the old Led Zeppelin song.

"Uh . . . I can't do it after school," I said. "I have to get home."

They both groaned with disappointment. But I didn't care.

I had to get home to check the diary. I had to see if another entry had appeared.

Would it be there, waiting for me? Waiting to tell me about tomorrow?

I saw Tessa watching me as I left school that afternoon. She was talking to another girl, but she had her eyes on me.

I didn't stop to talk to her.

I ran out the front doors and leaped down the front steps. It was a blustery, wintry day. Heavy, dark clouds covered the sky.

I was so eager to get home, I hadn't zipped my parka. As I ran, it billowed up behind me like a cape.

I'm a superhero! I thought. And what is my super-power? The ability to know the future!

The gusting wind helped to carry me the four blocks to my house. I felt as if I were flying.

I was half a block from home when I saw the little orange kitten dart into the street.

"Help! Get him! Get him!" a little red-faced boy came running frantically to the curb. I recognized him. Billy Miller, a kid I baby-sat for sometimes.

Billy's kitten was always running away.

Alex to the rescue! I thought. I was feeling like a superhero. I flew into the street, scooped up the kitten easily, spun around, and ran it back to Billy.

Billy was so happy to have the kitten back in his hands, he nearly squeezed it to death! He thanked me a hundred times and went running back to his house.

A few seconds later, I trotted up our gravel driveway. I stopped at the kitchen door. I swallowed hard, trying to catch my breath.

I had been feeling like a superhero. But now unpleasant thoughts forced their way into my mind.

The wind died, and my coat drooped around me. I suddenly felt as heavy as a rock.

Will the diary have an entry about tomorrow? I wondered.

Will it tell me the future every day?

Or was that some kind of accident or coincidence?

Why was that entry in the diary in the first place? And why was it written in my handwriting?

I didn't want to think about those two questions. They were kind of scary.

I crossed my fingers on both hands. "Please, please—show me another entry," I muttered.

Knowing the future was so totally cool. It meant that my grades were going to be better than ever. It meant that I could win a thousand bets with everyone! I could be *rich* by the end of the school year!

Rich! How sweet!

How totally sweet!

It meant that I'd never be broke again. It meant that I'd be a winner. A winner—and everyone would know it.

And . . . it meant that I'd always be *one day ahead of Tessa*.

I'd had the diary for only one day. One single day. But already I knew that I needed it.

Needed it!

My heart was racing as I tore open the back door and burst into the house. Clara, our housekeeper, was at the sink. I called "hi" to her and ran to the front stairs.

Then I pulled myself up the stairs two at a time.

I stumbled on the top step and nearly fell on my face. My backpack slid off my shoulders and bumped to the floor.

I didn't bother to pick it up.

I ran to my room.

And dove for the desk.

I pulled out the black leather diary.

"Please . . . please . . ." I muttered, gasping for breath.

I flipped open the cover. Gazed at the first page—the entry for today. So true. All of it, so true.

And what about tomorrow?

Breathing hard, I carefully turned to the next page.

I stared wide-eyed at the page. And let out a cry.

Nothing.

Nothing there.

I shuffled through the pages. All blank.

I closed the book and opened it again. But still the only entry was the first one.

I tossed the diary down and pounded my fists on the wooden desktop.

I felt so disappointed. As if someone had given me a really awesome Christmas present and then taken it away the next day.

I sat there for a few minutes, staring at the diary, trying to get over my disappointment. Then I dragged my backpack into my room and tried to do some math homework.

But it was hard to think about algebra.

Every five or ten minutes, I reached for the diary. And I opened it, hoping to find an entry about tomorrow.

At dinner, Mom and Dad were talking about going on a winter vacation to some island. They expected me to be excited about it.

But I barely heard a word they said. I kept thinking about the diary.

"Alex, are you feeling okay?" Mom asked, clearing my half-eaten dinner away. "You're very quiet tonight. That's not like you."

"I'm just thinking," I replied.

Dad laughed. "That's not like you either!" he joked.

Ha-ha.

I slid my chair back. "May I be excused?"

I didn't wait for an answer. I took off, running up the stairs to my room. I dove to the desk and grabbed the diary.

"Yes!" I cried happily. "Yes!" I did a wild dance around my room.

A new entry had appeared about tomorrow. Again, it was in my handwriting.

How is this happening? I asked myself. Is it some kind of strange magic? Do the new pages always arrive after dinner?

My hands were shaking from excitement. What is going to happen tomorrow?

I held the book steady in both hands and eagerly read:

DEAR DIARY,
   Wow! What a great day! Chip, Shawn, and I went to the basketball game after school. And it was amazing! The Ravens won in overtime!

Everyone in the gym went crazy. I thought they
were going to tear the building down!

"Whoa!" I murmured. My heart was pounding. I
read that first part again.

Our team will win in overtime tomorrow. And
then the diary gave me the final score of the game.

Wow!

I can win a few bets with *that* information!

If the diary tells me the score of every game
before it happens, I'll *never* lose another bet! I'll be
the richest kid in school!

And everyone will think I'm some kind of genius!

I turned back to the diary:

Tessa is suspicious about the geography test. I
saw her watching me. She is very curious about how I
did so well on the test when everyone else flunked.

I'm going to have to be a lot more careful around
Tessa. I don't want her to know about this diary.

She would ruin everything for me if she found out.
I know she would.

I heard a cough.

From behind me.

"Huh?" I turned quickly—and gasped.

Tessa stood in the doorway, scowling at me. Her
eyes were on the diary.

I slammed the book shut and shoved it into the top desk drawer. Then I jumped to my feet, ready to protect the diary from Tessa.

She stepped into the room, shaking her head. "I'm not interested in your stupid diary," she said. "You don't have to hide it, Alex. I wouldn't read it if you *paid* me!"

I let out a sigh of relief. But I didn't move away from the desk. I didn't trust her.

"I—I haven't started my diary entry for today yet," I said. That was *kind of* true. "I'm going to write it tonight."

"Don't bother," Tessa replied. "It won't be as good as mine."

"Why did you come over?" I asked. And then I flashed her an evil grin. "Need help with your geography homework?"

She groaned and narrowed her eyes at me. "How did you know about that test this morning, Alex?"

she asked. Her green eyes burned into mine.

"Uh . . . what makes you think I knew about it?" I said.

"You knew about it," she replied, still studying me. "You had to know about it. Or else you never would have passed it."

Wow! Tomorrow's diary entry is already coming true, I thought.

I crossed my arms over my chest. "That's stupid," I said. "How would I know about a surprise test?"

"That's what I'm asking you," she replied, tossing back her blond hair with a snap of her head. "Are you going to tell me?"

"I . . . just had a hunch," I replied. "Just a weird hunch. So I read over chapter eight last night. You know. Just in case my hunch was right."

She twisted up her heart-shaped lips and squinted hard at me. "A hunch?" She snickered. "You cheated somehow. I know you cheated. Did Mrs. Hoff tell you about the test in advance?"

"Huh?" I made a face at Tessa. "Why would Mrs. Hoff tell me anything? It was a wild hunch. Really."

I uncrossed my arms, feeling a little more relaxed. "Is that what you came over to ask me?"

Tessa seemed to relax too. "No. Not really . . ." She dropped down on the arm of a chair. "I was talking to Shawn. . . ."

"About what?"

"About your band," she said. "You see, I'm a really

good singer, and I've always wanted to sing with a band. And I know you guys don't have a singer. So—"

"You like to sing?" I interrupted. I couldn't picture it. Tessa was so stiff, so serious.

My stomach suddenly knotted in dread. Tessa wants to join our band. No! Please—no!

"I sing along to CDs all the time," she said. "And everyone says I'm very good. I'm really into pop, and I can sing oldies too. I've never tried rap, but—"

"Please!" I cried out. I couldn't help myself. The idea of Tessa singing rap made my stomach churn.

She jumped to her feet. "So do you think I could be in your band?"

"Well . . ." I swallowed hard. "Maybe," I said.

"Maybe?"

"I'll talk to Chip and Shawn. We'll take a vote or something. Then I'll let you know—okay?"

She seemed a little disappointed. She started to the door. "Okay," she said softly. "Thanks."

I couldn't wait for her to leave. As soon as I heard the door slam behind her, I pulled out the diary. And I read the entry about tomorrow five or six more times.

I memorized the score of tomorrow's Ravens game. And I made a plan for betting my friends on the game.

I was so excited, it took me a long time to fall asleep. When I finally drifted off, I dreamed about the diary.

I dreamed I was sitting at my desk. Thunder

roared outside, and lightning flashed in my bedroom window. The white light flickered in my room.

I lifted the diary from my desk drawer and began to read it by the flashing lightning.

In the dream, I turned the pages slowly. They were all filled in, but I didn't stop to read them.

Until I got to the last page.

Thunder boomed all around me. I raised the last page close to my face to read it.

And I saw one word on the page. Only one word, in bold black ink.

In the dream, I stared at the word as the lightning made it flicker on the page:

DEAD.

One word on the last page of the diary:

DEAD.

In my handwriting:

DEAD.

The dream ended in a blinding white flash of lightning.

I opened my eyes and sat straight up in bed.

Drenched with sweat, my pajamas stuck wetly to my skin.

Morning sunlight poured into the room. Mom stood at my bedroom doorway. She smiled at me. "Alex, you're already up? I came to wake you for school."

"Mom?" I asked, my voice hoarse from sleep. "Do dreams ever come true?"

"Move over," Chip boomed. He bumped me hard, forcing me to slide along the bleacher seat. Then he bumped me again, even harder, making me bounce into the guy next to me.

Chip laughed. He just likes bumping people. It's kind of his hobby.

The bleachers in the gym were filling up with kids and parents and a few teachers. Everyone cheered as the Ravens came running onto the floor in their black and gold uniforms, each player dribbling across the court.

The other team came running out of the visitor locker room. Their uniforms were yellow, and they were called the Hummingbirds.

Chip bumped me hard in the ribs with his elbow. "What a geeky name for a basketball team," he said. "The Hummingbirds."

"Yeah. Tweet-tweet," I said.

Shawn turned around from the bench below us.

"It's not so bad," he insisted. "Hummingbirds are very fast. And some people think they bring good luck."

Good old Shawn. He always has all the info.

Chip reached down and messed up Shawn's hair. Then he cupped his hands around his mouth and shouted at the Hummingbirds as they warmed up. "Tweet-tweet! Tweet-tweet!"

Some other kids laughed and joined in, until the chant spread across the gym.

The Hummingbirds were making most of their warm-up shots. One of their players was a giant. He had to be seven feet tall!

"Who is that guy?" I asked.

"His name is Hooper," Shawn said, turning around again.

Chip laughed. "He plays basketball and his name is Hooper? Cool!"

"He's only in seventh grade, and he's already six foot three," Shawn reported.

"Wow. He's a big Hummingbird!" I said.

A lot of kids laughed at that.

The game was about to start. I knew it was time to get serious.

"We're going to beat these birds," I said. "Anyone want to bet on it?"

Shawn turned around again. "Alex, you want to bet on the Ravens? Look at this guy Hooper. They're going to stuff us!"

"Yeah. This guy Hooper can block every shot," Chip said. "Look at him. He's a *tree!*"

A guy behind me tapped me on the shoulder. "You want to take the Ravens? I'll take the Hummingbirds. How much do you want to bet?"

"Yeah. I'll take the Hummingbirds too," Chip said. "Bet you five bucks."

This is too easy, I thought. Way too easy.

I had a plan. It was time to put it into gear.

"I don't want that bet," I said. "I want to do another kind of bet."

About a dozen kids were leaning in, listening to me now.

The referee's whistle echoed off the gym walls. Kids were cheering and shouting. The teams were gathering at center court.

"I'll bet anyone five dollars that this game goes into overtime," I announced.

"Huh?"

"Get serious!"

"Overtime? No way!"

I heard cries of disbelief all around.

"Alex, that's stupid," Shawn whispered. "Don't throw away your money."

"Who's got five dollars?" I called out. "Five dollars says the game goes into overtime. If it doesn't, I pay you five bucks."

More cries of disbelief. Guys were muttering that I'd totally lost it.

But ten kids took the bet. Ten times five. That's fifty bucks I was about to win.

If the diary's prediction came true . . .

I sat on the edge of the bench the entire game. My muscles were all tensed and I kept my hands clenched together in my lap.

The Hummingbirds got out to an early lead. The Ravens had a lot of trouble scoring because of Hooper. He stood under the basket and batted away just about every shot the Ravens took.

At halftime, the 'Birds were ahead by eight points. It looked pretty bad.

Chip, Shawn, and the other eight guys who bet against me all had big grins on their faces. "No way this game goes into overtime," Chip said, and he bumped me so hard, I fell into the aisle.

"We'll see," I said. But my stomach was doing flip-flops. I knew I didn't have fifty dollars to pay off the bet if I lost. In fact, I had only six dollars to my name.

The diary had to be right. Or else I was dead!
Dead.

The frightening dream suddenly flashed back into my mind. Once again I saw the single word written in big, bold script on the back page:

DEAD.

I blinked the picture away. Then I leaned forward and concentrated on the game, which had started up again.

The 'Birds scored first. Hooper hardly had to jump to slam-dunk the ball through the net.

I let out a groan. The Ravens were down by ten points now. If the game was going into overtime, they had to get to work.

I crossed my fingers on both hands and watched the game intently. I barely breathed. I kept seeing those ten guys with their hands stuck in my face, demanding their five dollars.

With a few minutes to go in the game, the Ravens had pulled to within two points. The seconds ticked by. The teams moved up and down the court.

A shot—and a miss.

A bad pass out of bounds.

Only a few seconds left. The Ravens had the ball. The kid with the ball drove right at Hooper. Hooper tripped. The Raven sent up a short layup.

Yes!

The Ravens tied the score at twenty-six just as the final buzzer went off. The game was going into overtime.

The gym practically exploded with cheers and startled cries. Kids stamped their feet so hard, the bleachers creaked and shook.

I leaped up and began jumping up and down on the bleacher floor. I pumped my fists in the air.

"Overtime! Overtime! I win! I win BIG-time!"

I went around and made everyone pay up. Ten times five. My biggest win ever.

How did it feel? Try *great*!

Chip was grumbling to Shawn. "This didn't happen," he muttered. "How could Alex know it would go into overtime?"

"So he got lucky once," Shawn replied.

Time for part two of my plan.

I stood up and turned to the guys who had bet me. "I'll give you a chance to win your money back," I announced. "I'll bet five dollars that the final score is 34 to 30, Ravens."

They were even more surprised at this bet. Some of them laughed really hard. The others just shook their heads.

"Come on, guys," I urged, "I'm giving you a chance. If the score isn't 34 to 30, I'll pay you back your money."

Only eight guys took this bet. The other two said they didn't have any more money to lose.

"You're crazy," Shawn told me. "You're totally whacked." But he took the bet anyway.

I sat back and concentrated on the game.

Would the diary come through again? So far, it had been totally right each time.

The overtime period was only five minutes. I didn't have long to wait.

Kids were screaming and cheering and stomping their feet. The game was tied at thirty. Then the Ravens scored two straight baskets right over Hooper's head.

Now the screams were so loud, I had to cover my ears with my hands.

I gazed at the scoreboard: 34 to 30, Ravens. Only five seconds left to play.

"Pay up, guys!" I shouted. "Check out the score! Alex the Great wins again!"

Out of the corner of my eye, I saw Hooper move to the basket. He sent up a long jump shot just as the buzzer rang out.

Swish! It dropped through!

Final score: Ravens, 34 to 32!

I lost the bet.

I paid the guys their money. They were laughing and goofing, slapping me on the back.

Chip kept chanting, "Alex the Great! Alex the Great!" He wrapped me in a headlock and rubbed his knuckles against the top of my head until my skull throbbed.

I finally pulled free and hurried down the bleacher steps. I saw Tessa watching me from the other bleacher. I waved to her, but I didn't stop.

I pushed through the crowd and made my way out of the school building. I had to get home to check the diary.

I ran all the way. I was totally out of breath, my right side aching, by the time I got to my room.

I pulled the diary from its drawer and turned to the second entry, the page for today.

I ran my finger down the page until I came to the final score of the basketball game. Yes. The final score in the diary was 34 to 32.

The diary had it right.

You see, I had deliberately lost the bet. I'd bet on the wrong score on purpose. I'd let them win.

The idea was to sucker them all.

I wanted them to think that I was crazy, that I didn't have a clue. So, the next time, they wouldn't be suspicious at all.

Next time, they'd take any bet I offered.

And I'd clean them out.

I closed the diary and gave the cover a big kiss.

I was feeling great.

Sure, I'd just lost big-time. I'd won fifty dollars, then lost forty.

But I was still ten dollars ahead. And there was plenty more where that came from. As long as the diary told the truth.

I'll be a millionaire by the end of the year, I thought.

A millionaire!

I didn't check the diary again until after dinner. That's when the new entries seemed to appear.

"Why do you keep grinning like that?" Dad asked. We were having ice cream sundaes for dessert. I didn't realize I was grinning.

I shrugged. "Just grinning."

"Who won the basketball game today?" he asked.

I wiped chocolate sauce from my chin. "We did. In overtime. It was awesome."

"I heard a rumor," Mom said, frowning at me. "I heard that kids in your school have been betting on the basketball games. Is that true?"

I swallowed a lump of ice cream. "That's dumb," I said.

Mom squinted at me. "The rumor is dumb? Or betting on the games is dumb?"

"Both," I said.

I don't like to lie to my parents. I always try to be as honest as I can.

"The school should clamp down on kids who bet," Dad said, squirting more Reddi-wip on his ice cream. "You're too young for that."

Mom kept staring at me. Did she suspect something? Did someone tell her that I was the one making the bets?

I grinned at her. "Bet you ten dollars the school catches those kids!" I said.

Mom and Dad both burst out laughing. When things start to get tense, I can always make them laugh.

I finished my sundae and hurried up to my room to read the diary.

Would it tell me about tomorrow?

As I opened the diary, my hands shook with excitement.

This was so totally cool! Knowing things that no one else knew was just about the most awesome thing that could happen!

Little did I realize as I began to scan the words in the entry for tomorrow . . . little did I realize that sometimes knowing things can be really bad news.

I was so excited, the words kept blurring on the page.

I took a deep breath and held it to calm myself down. Then I started to read the entry—in my handwriting—moving my finger over the page, word by word.

DEAR DIARY,

Here is a big surprise. Tessa is in the band! I told her she could join. Chip and Shawn were really upset about it. They didn't want Tessa anywhere near our band. They didn't even want her to listen to the band! But then I explained to them why I let her in.

You see, Tessa told me about her uncle Jon. Uncle Jon has a big garage that's mostly empty. He told Tessa the band could rehearse there.

He's Tessa's favorite uncle, and I can understand why.

You see, Uncle Jon owns a restaurant downtown.

And he told Tessa that if we rehearse a lot, and if he thinks our band is good enough, he'll let us play at his restaurant! And he says he'll pay us!

I had no choice. I couldn't turn that down. I had to let Tessa into the band.

Such awesome news! I wanted to call Chip and Shawn and tell them about it.

But I couldn't tell them until Tessa told me. I had to keep things in the right order. Or else I'd get totally messed up and confused.

I returned to the diary to see what else was going to happen tomorrow . . .

Mrs. Culter was out sick. Everyone in her algebra class was really happy at first. They all thought that meant they wouldn't have the algebra test.

But then the substitute teacher came in with the algebra test. And we had to take it anyway.

I'd better study the algebra problems really hard tonight, I decided. Algebra is my worst subject. Having this info about the test tomorrow was really helpful.

There was one more entry in the diary. I leaned over the little book to read it—when the phone rang.

I let out a groan. I didn't want to talk to anyone. I wanted to finish learning about tomorrow.

I jerked the telephone off the desktop and raised

it to my ear. "Hello?"

"Hi, Alex." I recognized Tessa's voice instantly. "What are you doing?" she asked.

"Uh . . . working on my diary," I said. "I really don't have time to talk. This is the best diary entry I've ever written. Miss Gold is going to go nuts when she reads it!"

Tessa laughed. "At least you're modest."

"I've got to go," I said.

"Well, I just want to ask one question," Tessa replied. "Can I be in the band or not? Did you talk to Chip and Shawn?"

"Yes," I told her. "You can be in the band, Tessa. If you really can sing."

"Yay!" she cheered. "You won't be sorry, Alex. Really. I'm good. And guess what?"

I'll bet I can guess, I thought.

"I talked to my uncle Jon. And he may have a place for us to rehearse."

"That's great!" I exclaimed, trying to sound surprised.

"Uncle Jon wants to hear us," Tessa said. "He says if we're good enough, we can play at his restaurant."

"Cool," I said.

"Maybe I could come over tonight, and we could work on some songs together," Tessa said.

I made a disgusted face at the phone. "No. Not tonight," I told her. "I can't. I have to study for the algebra test."

"Don't bother," Tessa replied.

"Huh? Don't bother? What do you mean?" I asked.

"Mrs. Culter is sick," Tessa replied. "She came to see my mom at her office this afternoon."

Tessa's mom is a doctor.

"Mom says that Mrs. Culter is really sick," Tessa continued. "She won't be back in school for at least the rest of the week. So . . . no way we'll have the algebra test tomorrow."

I almost burst out laughing. I had to smack a hand over my mouth to keep silent.

"That's great news," I managed to choke out.

"I've been calling everyone and telling them the test is off," Tessa said.

"Cool!" I exclaimed.

I held my hand over the phone and let out a wild giggle. I couldn't hold it back.

That's one more test that I'll ace, I told myself. And one more test that Tessa will flunk!

I felt so happy, I *kissed* the diary!

It took me a few more minutes to get Tessa off the phone. When I finally hung up, I jumped to my feet. And I did another crazy dance around my room.

"Tessa flunks!" I chanted, pumping my fists in the air. "Tessa flunks! Tessa flunks!"

Poor Tessa, I thought. She just doesn't have the right diary. She doesn't have a diary that can tell her the future.

I suddenly remembered I hadn't finished tomorrow's entry. There was still one last sentence to read.

I felt so happy, almost giddy, as I picked up the diary from my desk.

But my mood changed as my eyes swept over the last sentence in tomorrow's entry.

I gasped—and squinted at the words in disbelief . . .

Bad news, diary. On my way home from school, I was hit by a car.

"No!"

I let out a cry. "No way!"

I stared at the words. I blinked a few times, then read them again:

On my way home from school, I was hit by a car.

"That is *so* not going to happen," I said out loud.

The diary must have made a mistake. I'm a really careful guy. I never run out in the street without looking.

Why did it say that?

How could it be wrong when it had been right about everything else?

I slammed the book shut and slid it into the desk drawer.

My heart was pounding. I'll just have to be careful tomorrow, I told myself. I'll just have to be super careful—and make sure the diary prediction doesn't come true.

Last night's frightening dream suddenly flashed

into my mind.

DEAD. . . . The one word glowing in bold black ink in the diary. DEAD. . . .

Is it going to come true?

The diary only says I get hit by a car, I told myself, tapping my fingers nervously on the desktop.

It doesn't say how badly I get hurt. Or if . . . if I die.

Why doesn't it say? Why does it stop there?

Why doesn't it tell me what happens?

I swallowed hard.

Is it because *there's nothing more to tell?*

I jerked open the desk drawer and pulled out the diary.

Maybe it will tell me more, I thought. Maybe it will tell me if I'm going to be okay.

My hands were so sweaty, the pages stuck to my fingers. I finally turned to tomorrow's entry and read it again.

Bad news, diary. On my way home from school, I was hit by a car.

Nothing more. Nothing.

Mom came to wake me for school at seven the next morning. I groaned and rolled over.

"I have an upset stomach," I moaned. "It hurts. I really feel sick."

Mom bit her bottom lip. She leaned over my bed and pressed her hand over my forehead. "You don't feel hot. Should I call Dr. Owens?" she asked.

"No. I just need to sleep," I whispered, doing my

best sick act. "I think I'd better stay home today."

I'd thought about this plan all night. If I stayed home, there was no way I could be hit by a car.

"Well, okay," Mom said, frowning at me, studying my eyes. "I'll make you some hot tea. It might settle your stomach."

I nodded weakly. I listened to her make her way back downstairs.

I settled my head into the pillow. You're pretty smart, Alex, I told myself. Stay home all day, and the diary will have to be wrong.

The phone rang. I picked it up and clicked it on. "Hello?" I asked weakly.

"Don't forget your guitar. Are you *psyched*? I'm totally psyched!"

It was Chip. What was he so excited about?

"My guitar?" I croaked. "What—?"

"You didn't forget!" he exclaimed. "You couldn't forget that the three of us are playing in the lunchroom today."

Oh, wow.

I did forget. I was so busy worrying about the diary.

Mrs. Jarvis, the lunchroom supervisor, said we could play for everyone at lunchtime. Our first time in public!

"Can you bring your amp?" Chip asked. "We can set up during study hall."

"Uh . . . yeah. Sure," I replied.

I couldn't let my friends down. I had no choice. I had to go to school.

And, of course, there was the algebra test first period. A test I was ready to ace.

Okay, okay. I'm going, I decided, climbing to my feet.

I'll just be careful after school, I decided. Real careful . . .

When I arrived at school carrying my guitar and amp, I had a surprise in store. Chip and Shawn were not glad to see me. In fact, they were totally steamed.

They came stomping toward me, swinging their fists tensely at their sides. I set the equipment down and turned to face them.

Chip bumped me hard with his chest, so hard I went sprawling against the wall of lockers.

"Hey—good morning to you too!" I said, trying to click my shoulder back into place.

"Why did you tell Tessa she can be in the band?" Shawn demanded.

"Yeah. Why?" Chip repeated. He bumped me again, a little harder. "Are you crazy?"

"Guys, give me a break," I pleaded. I raised both hands in front of me as a shield.

"We don't want Tessa in the band," Shawn said.

"We don't like Tessa," Chip added.

"I know, I know," I said. I dodged away from another bump from Chip.

"But it's going to work out," I told them. "You'll see. We'll be glad about it."

"Have you lost it?" Chip demanded. "She says she's going to sing with us at lunch. And we haven't even rehearsed with her."

"No problem," I said. "Did Tessa tell you about her uncle Jon?"

"We don't care about her uncle," Chip said angrily. "We don't want her messing up our band."

"Did she *pay* you?" Shawn asked. "How much did she pay you, Alex?"

"She didn't," I said. "I promise. It'll work out, guys. Her uncle is going to give us our first big break."

"We have to talk about this," Shawn said, shaking his head. "I know we need a singer. But—Tessa?"

"I can't talk now," I said, trying to push past them. "I've got my algebra test first thing." I grabbed my stuff and took off, running down the hall.

"Didn't you hear?" Shawn called after me. "Culter is out sick. No test today!"

But of course he was wrong and the diary was right.

You should have heard the other kids groan and moan when the substitute passed out the test papers.

I watched Tessa turn bright red. Tears filled her eyes.

She lowered her head and wouldn't look at anyone. She was so embarrassed!

She had called everyone and told them not to study.

Ha-ha. I couldn't keep the grin off my face as I breezed through the test.

Score another victory for Alex the Great!

I finished early and took my test paper up to the substitute. I flashed Tessa a big thumbs-up as I walked back to my seat.

She scowled and turned away. I could see that her test paper was a mess.

I dropped back into my seat, feeling really good about myself.

Our band was excited at lunchtime.

Chip, Shawn, and I set up our amps at a side of the lunchroom. Tessa brought a list of songs she knew, and there were a few on the list the three of us could play.

We started to tune up. Tessa kept clearing her throat. "I'm a little nervous," she confessed, "since we've never rehearsed or anything."

"Don't worry," I told her. "You'll be fine."

But she wasn't fine.

In fact, she was *horrible*!

Chip, Shawn, and I played "Purple Haze" to get things started. It's our best song, and the kids in the lunchroom seemed to like it. A few kids even clapped.

Then Tessa stepped up to sing. But she didn't sing—she screeched! Her singing sounded like fingernails being scraped down a chalkboard! Only more painful.

She sounded like a wounded animal howling in pain. She couldn't hit a single note. I couldn't even tell what song she was singing.

Kids stopped eating and started to beg for her to stop. That made Tessa sing even louder. I saw some kids running out of the lunchroom. One boy stuck his finger down his throat and pretended to puke.

We were supposed to play for half an hour. But Mrs. Jarvis stopped us after Tessa's first song. "Good work," she said. "Pack up quickly—okay?"

As we packed up, Chip and Shawn scowled angrily at me.

But Tessa seemed really cheerful. "That wasn't bad. But I'll get even better," she said, smiling at me. "I just need to rehearse a little."

"She embarrassed us for life," Chip muttered sadly as we carried our guitars down the hall. "How could you let her in our band?"

I didn't answer. I had other things to think about. Mainly, the diary.

Why didn't the diary say that Tessa was the worst singer in history? Why did it leave out that part?

When her uncle Jon hears her sing, he won't let us anywhere near his restaurant! I thought bitterly. Why didn't the diary tell me that?

What else did the diary leave out about today? I wondered. What else?

I felt a shiver of fear. I kept picturing myself hit by a car . . . flying into the air . . . flattened, crushed, mangled, wrecked.

Was it going to come true? Was I a few hours away from my DOOM?

"Let's get our bikes and go up to the dirt-bike track," Chip suggested after school. He slapped a heavy arm around my shoulders. "How about it, Alex?"

"I—I don't think so," I said quietly.

It was a cool, sunny afternoon. A tag football game had already started on the playground. Kids were running with their open jackets flapping behind them.

Everyone was laughing and shouting, happy to be out of school.

I didn't feel like laughing. My throat felt tight, and my stomach was doing flip-flops. I wanted to walk home slowly and carefully, and hide there till the day was over.

"Yeah, let's go!" Shawn said. "The track is empty during the week. We'll have it all to ourselves."

Chip laughed at him. "You'll have to take your training wheels off first!"

"Give me a break," Shawn muttered. He tried to shove Chip, but Chip danced away.

"I can't do it today," I said.

I turned and gazed down the street.

Was there a car out there with my name on it? Was there a car on its way right now, roaring down the street, coming to nail me?

With a shudder, I turned back to my friends. "Here's another idea. Why don't you guys bring your guitars to my house, and we'll practice some new songs."

Chip grinned at me. "We can't practice without Tessa, your *girlfriend*—can we?" he asked in a high, teasing voice.

Shawn laughed. "Alex and Tessa. What a gruesome twosome!"

I rolled my eyes. "You two are *so* not funny. Come on. Maybe Tessa was just nervous. Maybe we can teach her to be a better singer."

"Yeah. Maybe if we tape her mouth shut," Chip muttered.

They finally agreed to come over. But they said they had to stop at their houses first.

I turned and started walking toward home. I kept on the grass beside the sidewalk, as far from the street as I could get.

My legs trembled as I walked. My heart was racing in my chest.

"Don't be dumb. There's nothing to be scared

about," I told myself. "Two more blocks and you're home."

I walked slowly, carefully, keeping my eyes straight ahead.

I was half a block from home when I saw the little orange kitten run into the street.

"Not again!" I cried.

I heard Billy Miller's screams before I saw him come darting out from behind a hedge. "My kitten! My kitten!"

I glimpsed Billy's frightened face. I saw the little cat freeze in the center of the intersection.

I had no choice.

I had to rescue it.

I leaped into the street and started to run.

"My kitten! Alex—help! Get my kitten!"

Running hard, I heard the blast of a car horn. Then the shrill squeal of tires on the pavement.

"Uhh."

I felt a hard bump. From behind.

My hands flew up.

And I was flying, flying through the air.

I flew into a bright white light. The street, the lawns, the sky—they all disappeared.

All colors vanished. I seemed to fly forever.

I landed in a shock of pain. The world rushed back. Colors and sounds.

I heard Billy crying. A car door slammed. A woman shouted, "Hey! Hey! Hey!" The same word over and over.

The sky spun above me, whirled so fast, as if I were on some kind of amusement park ride.

"Hey! Hey!"

The woman bent over me, her face red and twisted in fear. "Hey—are you all right?"

My skin prickled. Something scratched my arms. Blinking, I realized I had landed on a thick evergreen bush.

I struggled to catch my breath. I gazed up at the frightened woman.

"Are you all right? I—I almost stopped in time. I didn't hit you hard, but—"

"I . . . think I'm okay," I said. The sky stopped spinning above me. I saw Billy holding the kitten in his arms.

With a groan, I sat up. I pulled bristles off my arms and the front of my shirt. The bush had cradled my fall.

"Does anything hurt?" the woman asked. "Is anything broken? Should I call the police? An ambulance? Can you stand up?"

"I . . . think so," I said. She helped pull me up.

I felt shaky but okay. I tested my arms, my legs. I twisted my head around. Everything checked out okay. Nothing broken, nothing hurting.

"I'm so sorry," the woman said, her voice trembling. "I almost stopped in time. I . . . I just feel so awful."

I pulled more pine needles off my jacket. "It's okay," I told her. "I knew I was going to be hit by a car today."

Her frightened expression faded. She narrowed her eyes at me.

I knew instantly that I'd said the wrong thing. The words had just spilled out.

She studied me intently. "We'd better get you to a doctor," she said.

Mom and Dad took me to see Dr. Owens. She checked me out and said everything was all right. "You might feel a little stiff and sore tomorrow," she said. "But I think you can go to school."

Wow. Hit by a car, and I don't even get a day off from school!

On the way home, I slumped in the back of the car, feeling really glum. What a lost opportunity, I thought bitterly. I really blew it this time.

What if I had made a bet with Chip and Shawn? What if I'd bet them that I'd be hit by a car on the way home?

I could have won big-time!

"You were really lucky," Mom said, turning from the passenger seat to face me. "Really lucky."

No, I wasn't, I thought. What's lucky about being hit by a car and not winning a dime from it?

"Next time, Alex, look both ways before running out to save a kitten," Dad said.

Ha-ha. Very funny.

Chip, Shawn, and Tessa were waiting in the driveway when I got home. They cheered when I told them I was perfectly okay.

But Tessa tilted her head and stared hard at me.

"Alex, I know why you ran out into the street and got hit by a car today," she said.

"I do too," I replied. "To rescue a kitten."

She shook her head. "No. To make sure your diary is more interesting than mine. You'll do *anything* to win our bet!"

Chip and Shawn laughed. But I didn't think it was funny.

"I don't have to do a lot of crazy things to make my diary interesting," I told Tessa. "Because I'm a really good writer."

So far, of course, I hadn't written a single word in the diary. The diary had written it all for me.

Thinking about the diary gave me a chill.

What would it say about tomorrow? Would it have more bad news for me?

I suddenly realized I was afraid of the diary. I was so excited at first. But knowing the future was really creepy.

Maybe I shouldn't open it again, I thought. Maybe I should tuck the thing away in a drawer and never look at it again.

But would that change things?

Wouldn't the same things happen in my life even if I didn't read about them first in the diary?

"I talked to my uncle Jon." Tessa's words broke into my thoughts. "He says his garage is ready. We can use it anytime to rehearse in."

"Yaay! That is totally awesome news!" Chip

exclaimed. "Let's go right now!"

"I can't," I said. "I was just in an accident—remember?"

Chip nodded. "Oh, yeah. Right."

We made a plan to try to rehearse that weekend. Then, feeling sore and achy, I made my way into the house for dinner.

A noisy thunderstorm struck while we were eating. Lightning crackled over the backyard, and a boom of thunder made the house shake. Rain poured down. The lights flickered but didn't go out.

Mom and Dad kept glancing at me as I ate. I knew they were thinking about the car hitting me. But none of us talked about it.

After dinner, I hurried upstairs to my room. I slid the diary out from its hiding place in my desk drawer. Then, holding it between my hands, I stared at the cover.

I didn't open it. I wondered if I could keep myself from opening it.

My hands trembled as I held it. I was afraid of it now—and I had good reason to be.

I knew I was holding some kind of magic. But was it *evil* magic?

Diary, what is your secret? I wondered for the hundredth time. How do you know what's going to happen tomorrow?

And why are you written in my handwriting?

My hands moved as if on their own. As if I were

no longer in control.

My hands pried open the diary.

I shuffled through the pages.

Yes. There it was—an entry for tomorrow.

I didn't want to read it. I didn't want to know.

But I couldn't help myself.

I raised the book close to my face and started to read.

DEAR DIARY,

The eighth-graders had their Junior Olympics at the running track in back of school today. The track was still wet from all the rain last night. Runners kept slipping and falling, and a couple of kids really cut up their knees.

The wind was blowing like a hurricane. Some of the javelin throwers had their javelins come flying back at them! It was a mess, but we seventh-graders got out of school all day to watch them. So we thought it was terrific.

The blue team won every single event. Except for the broad jump, which was a tie.

"Excellent!" I cried out loud. I set the diary down and pumped my fist above my head.

I hope Chip and Shawn and the other guys bring lots of money to school tomorrow! I'm going to win it all! All!

They won't believe that Blue can win every event. And then, when I bet them the broad jump is a tie, I'll clean them out!

Thinking about all the bets I would win really cheered me up. I could forgive the diary for the car accident. I suddenly didn't feel as scared of it. The little book was going to make me rich!

I raised it close and began to read the rest of tomorrow's entry. . . .

> Tessa keeps giving me a hard time. I can't tell if she is teasing me or not.
>
> She keeps saying that I'm doing things just to make my diary more interesting than hers. She says I'll do anything to win our bet.
>
> It isn't true at all. But what is Tessa going to think when she hears the crazy thing I did after school?

Huh? After school?

My heart started to pound. As I gripped the diary, my hands were suddenly cold and wet.

What did I do after school?

I bent over the diary and read. . . .

> You should have heard the screams. Everyone was in a total panic.
>
> Maybe a hundred kids were watching me, and more were running over from the playground.

I heard kids shouting all down the block and out to the street.

What an adventure!

I don't even remember climbing up onto the roof of the school building. But there I was, teetering on the roof edge at the gutter.

And then, it's hard to believe—but I did it. I flapped my arms like a bird and jumped off the roof.

"Ten . . . fifteen . . . twenty . . ."

After the Junior Olympics, I stayed in the bleachers to count the money I had won. The total came to thirty-five dollars.

Not a bad day's work.

I jammed the wad of fives into my jeans pocket and zipped my denim jacket up to my chin. I shivered.

What a cold, dreary day. The sky had been dull and gray all afternoon. The ground was still drenched from the heavy rains last night.

A cold wind kept gusting, swirling, blowing so hard, the bleachers behind the school trembled.

Leaning into the wind, I made my way into the school building. I had spent all afternoon watching the Junior Olympics. Cashing in big-time.

Now I had to pick up my backpack from my locker and walk home.

Walk home *without* climbing up onto the roof of the school.

This is one diary prediction that will not come true, I decided.

I waved to Tessa, who stood talking to a group of girls.

Tessa made a face and turned away from me. She was steamed because she lost ten dollars to me betting that the broad jump *wouldn't* be a tie.

Ha-ha. My diary is better than yours! I thought.

I had been thinking about the diary all day.

Of course, I didn't understand it. I didn't understand how it worked, how it knew the future.

It was kind of magical. It was totally scary.

But, so far, finding it was the best thing that had ever happened to me.

The next Ravens basketball game is tomorrow, I suddenly remembered. I know the score of the game will be waiting for me in tomorrow's diary entry.

I could feel the wad of five-dollar bills in my jeans. Maybe I'll let the guys win a few dollars at first, I thought. Just so they don't get suspicious when I totally clean them out again.

Yes, the diary was definitely great. Awesome. Fantastic.

If only it didn't bring any more bad news.

I felt a cold tingle of fear. Was the diary also evil?

I stopped in front of my locker. I shivered again. A frightening thought rolled through my mind.

What if the diary was *causing* these bad things to happen?

What if it wasn't just reporting what happened the next day? What if it was *causing* me to be hit by a car? What if the diary *forced* me to jump off the roof?

No. No way.

I shook my head hard, as if trying to shake that thought from my mind.

What a crazy idea.

That little book can't force me to do anything, I decided.

I am a free person. I have a mind of my own. I can decide what to do and what not to do.

No book can tell *me* what to do!

I swung my backpack over my shoulders and jogged out the back door of the school. The sky was even darker. Another storm was on its way. The air felt cold and wet.

I saw a couple of guys tossing a football back and forth at the edge of the playground. Their shoes sloshed in the wet grass. The gusting wind kept carrying the football out of their hands.

I turned away from the school. A blast of wind sent my hair flying straight up. I brushed it down with both hands. Then, leaning into the wind, I started toward home.

I had gone only two or three steps, when I heard the screams.

Frantic screams.

"Alex—help me! Help!"

I froze at the sound of my name.

"Alex! Alex! Help me!"

I uttered a startled gasp and spun around.

A little boy stood in the grass near the back of the building, waving frantically.

I took a few steps toward him and his face came into focus. Billy Miller.

Not again!

"Alex—help!"

I took off running. "Where's your cat?" I cried.

Some other kids were also hurrying over to Billy. The two boys dropped their football and came running. I saw two of Tessa's friends trotting to help the boy.

I got to him first. "Where's your cat?" I repeated breathlessly. My eyes searched the playground.

"At home," Billy said. The wind blew his blond hair over his face.

I gaped at him. "Huh? At home?"

"It's not my kitten!" he wailed. "It's my Raiders cap! My new Raiders cap! Look!"

He stuck his arm up, pointing wildly. "Up there. The wind blew it!"

"Oh, noooo," I moaned. I raised my eyes to the slanted, black roof of the school. Squinting into the gray sky, I could see the black-and-silver Raiders cap. It rested on the rain gutter at the edge of the roof.

I'm not going up there to get it, I told myself.

I'm not going to make that diary entry come true.

I turned back to Billy. He had tears in his eyes. His face was bright red. His bottom lip kept quivering. "Please?" he whispered. "It's my brand-new cap."

What is up with this kid? I wondered. It's like he is *haunting* me! He already caused me to get hit by a car.

And now . . .

"Maybe the wind will blow it back down," I told Billy. "Maybe if you wait long enough . . ."

"NOOOO!" he wailed. "I WANT IT! I WANT MY CAP!"

"Get it for him, Alex," Nella, one of Tessa's friends, shouted. "Just climb up the drainpipe. It's not hard."

"Uh . . . I'm not a good climber," I said. "I . . . don't have the right shoes."

"Help the poor kid," another girl said. "Look at

him—he's crying!"

Tears were streaming down Billy's cheeks. He still had his hand raised, pointing to the cap.

"Maybe someone else could help," I said. I turned to the crowd of kids who had gathered around us. I counted at least twenty kids. "Does anyone else like to climb?"

"Help him, Alex," Nella repeated. "Just shinny up the drainpipe. It's not that high."

"Any volunteers?" I pleaded. "Anyone?"

No one.

"I WANT MY RAIDERS CAP!" Billy shrieked.

I swallowed hard. I gazed at the metal drainpipe running up the side of the building to the rain gutter along the edge of the roof. "Okay, okay," I muttered.

I had no choice. Everyone was staring at me. If I just left Billy standing there crying, no one would ever let me forget it.

So . . . I was doing it. I was heading up to the roof.

Kids clapped and cheered. I stepped up to the wall and grabbed the metal drainpipe with both hands.

It felt wet and slippery from all the rain. The wind blew, making the gutter above me rattle.

I gazed straight up. The building was only two stories high at this end. But the roof appeared a mile above me!

I could see the cap. It was hanging halfway over the gutter edge.

If only a gust of wind would blow it down and save me from having to do this!

But . . . no.

I took a deep breath and grasped the cold, wet drainpipe. I moved my hands high and wrapped my legs around the pipe.

Kids were still cheering, urging me on. I glimpsed Billy standing in front of the crowd. He had finally stopped crying. He had his eyes raised to the cap.

With a groan, I pulled myself up. My hands slipped on the wet metal. But I kept a tight grip on the pipe with my legs.

Slowly, slowly, I pulled myself up.

I was gasping for breath when I reached the roof. I leaned forward carefully and spread my hands onto the dark shingles. Then I pulled myself onto the roof.

The roof seemed to slant straight up. One slip, I realized, and I could roll right off.

I was on my hands and knees on the edge of the roof. A strong wind fluttered my jacket.

My whole body was trembling. My legs felt like rubber. I started to crawl forward. So carefully. Planting one hand. Then the other. Sliding one knee forward. Then the other knee.

The Raiders cap was only a few yards away. But I kept slipping on the wet shingles, sliding toward the edge of the roof.

Each time I slipped, a scream went up from the kids below. I turned and glimpsed other kids running from the playground.

I could hear their excited shouts. I knew they were cheering me on. But I couldn't make out their words.

I crawled forward, inch by inch. And then I stretched out one hand . . . stretched . . .

. . . and grabbed the cap.

Below, kids were cheering and shouting, slapping high-fives. Billy leaped into the air, laughing and clapping.

"Yes!" I cried, gripping the cap tightly in my fist. "Yes!" I jumped to my feet.

Why?

Why did I jump to my feet?

It was as if I had lost control. Some kind of powerful force had pulled me up.

There I was, standing on the edge of the roof, laughing, waving the cap in the air. A victory celebration?

No! I didn't want to be there. What had pulled me to the roof edge?

I lowered the cap to my side. And stared down, gripped with cold, sudden horror.

So far down to the ground.

What next? What next? I asked myself.

My whole body shuddered.

Am I going to flap my arms and jump off? Just as the diary said?

Is there nothing I can do to save myself?

The diary—it's always right, I realized to my horror. It always tells the truth.

And if it says I jump off the roof . . .

I'm going to break my neck. Or worse. Because the diary is . . . in control.

Trembling in the strong wind, I glanced down at the crowd again. The kids had grown silent. They all stared up at me tensely. No one moved.

I stared down at them, my mind swirling like the wind.

"Get down!" someone shouted.

"Alex—be careful!" I heard Nella cry.

"Alex—back up! Get back!"

Maybe I can make big bucks from this jump, I suddenly thought. If I'm going to break all my bones, at least maybe I can win a few bets.

I cupped my hands around my mouth and shouted down to them. "Does anyone dare me to jump?"

The wind blew the words back at me. And before anyone down below could reply, my shoes started to slide on the wet shingles.

"No—!" I gasped.

My arms flew up in the air as I lost my balance.

My legs slid out from under me.

My hands flapped wildly in the air.

One shoe caught in the gutter. The other slid over the edge.

I heard shrill screams. A rush of cold wind.

And flailing, kicking, and thrashing, I fell.

The ground shot up to meet me.

It looked like a video game. All bright colors and screaming sound, and everything happening in jagged slow motion.

And then I saw a figure shooting forward. An alarmed face.

Arms straight out.

A hard *thud*.

I bounced. Bounced in someone's arms.

Colors swirled around me. And the screams—the screams all around, so shrill, I thought my ears would burst.

"Huh?" I uttered a choked cry as I realized some-one had caught me.

A teacher. Mrs. Walker, the art teacher. I landed hard on top of her. We both tumbled to the grass. She let out a groan, then struggled to untangle herself from me.

How embarrassing, I thought, still dizzy, still falling

in my mind. Still feeling the ground rushing up to me.

How embarrassing. Caught by a teacher.

"Alex, are you okay?" she asked breathlessly, climbing shakily to her feet.

I jumped up quickly. "Fine," I said, trying to shake off the dizziness. "Fine . . . I guess."

Mrs. Walker let out a sigh. She brushed off her jacket. Then tested her arms. "You should go on a diet if you're going to jump off buildings."

Lots of kids laughed. I forced a smile.

Mrs. Walker's expression changed. "What on earth were you doing up there?"

"Billy's cap," I murmured. "I had to bring down his cap. . . ."

Where was it? What happened to the cap?

I glanced around. And saw a black-and-silver Raiders cap pulled down low over Billy's head. A big grin beneath the cap.

Billy was happy.

For the second time in one week, he had almost gotten me killed! And there he was, grinning his head off.

"That was really dangerous," Mrs. Walker said.

I nodded. "Yes, I know."

My whole life has become dangerous, I thought. My whole life is one frightening moment after another.

All because of the diary.

I picked up my backpack and started for home. Kids slapped me high-fives and congratulated me.

"Way to go, Alex!"

"That was totally cool!"

But I didn't feel totally cool. And I didn't feel like celebrating.

I wanted to hurry home and think. I had to think hard about this. Should I keep the diary? Or should I throw it in the trash?

Could I throw it in the trash?

No. No . . . it had a powerful hold on me, I realized.

I needed it. I needed to know what would happen next.

I couldn't fight it. I had tried to fight what it said. I had tried to make the diary wrong.

But it was always right. Always.

I burst into the house and tossed down my backpack. Then I leaped up the stairs two at a time.

I dove into my room. My heart pounding, I crossed to my desk.

Jerked open the drawer.

Reached for the diary. Reached for it.

"Huh?" I uttered a sharp cry.

Panic choked my throat.

My hand fumbled through the drawer. I pulled the drawer out all the way.

And stared down.

Stared wide-eyed.

Gone.

The diary was gone!

I heard someone laugh.

Startled, I spun around.

Chip and Shawn sat on my bed, grinning. Chip waved the diary at me.

"Hey—!" I cried. "Where'd you get that?"

Chip's grin grew wider. He pointed. "On your desk. Shawn and I are going to read your deep, dark secrets."

"No!" I screamed. "Give it back!" I dove across the room and made a grab for it.

Chip giggled and dodged away from me. He tossed the diary to Shawn.

Shawn jumped to his feet and ran to the door.

"Come on—!" I shouted. "Give it!" I leaped at Shawn. Tackled him around the waist.

As I pulled him to the floor, he heaved the diary back to Chip. Chip reached for it—but it flew over his hand and bounced off the wall, onto the bed.

Chip and I dove for it, scrambling. I shoved him

hard. "Give it back to me!" I shrieked. "I mean it! Give it back!"

Then I totally lost it. I jumped on top of him and began pounding him with my fists. "Give it back! Give it back!"

Stunned, Chip rolled away. He dropped onto the floor and stared up at me in surprise. "Okay, okay," he muttered. "It's just a stupid diary."

I grabbed the little book and squeezed it tightly in my hand. I struggled to catch my breath. My heart was pounding.

"What is your problem, Alex?" Shawn asked, shaking his head. "We weren't going to hurt your diary."

"You didn't have to go totally berserk," Chip added.

"What's in that diary anyway?" Shawn asked. "Did you write stuff about *us* in there?"

"No," I said. "No way." I tucked the diary into the desk drawer and pushed the drawer shut. "I just . . . don't like people messing with my stuff."

"We're not people," Shawn replied, eyeing me intently. "We're your friends!"

"I know, but—"

"Forget about the diary," Chip said. He grabbed my arm and used me to pull himself to his feet. "Let's hang out or something. We could try those new video games you got."

"Uh . . . I can't," I said. "I've got to . . . uh . . . go

somewhere with my parents tonight. So I have to do my homework now."

They both stared at me. Could they tell I was lying?

I didn't want to hang out with them. I wanted to see the new diary entry. I wanted to sit and think about the diary.

They had given me a bad scare. When the diary wasn't in its right place, I totally freaked. Now I knew—I needed the diary. *Needed* it!

But I couldn't explain it to them. I couldn't really explain it to myself.

As soon as they left, I pulled the diary from the desk and eagerly shuffled through the pages. No new entry yet. I read over the old ones.

True. Everything in it was true. Every prediction had been exactly right.

I didn't know how it was happening. Or why. But as I stared at the blank pages, waiting for them to fill up with the next entry, I knew that I couldn't *live* without this book. I hated it—and I needed it at the same time.

After dinner, the next entry was waiting for me in the diary. But it was an entry I wished I hadn't read. An entry I didn't want to believe.

First, it gave me the score of tomorrow's Ravens game. Very handy.

But the rest of the entry filled me with dread:

After the basketball game, Shawn was riding his bike home. It was a cloudy, foggy evening, and Shawn was going really fast to get home before the rain started.

He wasn't looking where he was going. And I saw him crash. I saw the whole thing.

He smashed head-on into a parked truck. Poor Shawn. He flipped up into the air. He landed hard. Knocked unconscious. And he broke his leg in two places.

"No way!" I cried out loud, staring until the words blurred on the page. "No way. I won't let this happen. I *can't* let this happen."

The diary entries were becoming more and more frightening. Each prediction was more terrifying than the last.

But I can stop this one, I decided. I can stop it from happening.

Can't I?

"Hey, Shawn, want to walk home with me after the basketball game?"

A cheer rang out as the Ravens scored. They were winning 35 to 25. Once again, the diary was right on target. I was about to win forty dollars from my friends.

"I can't. I rode my bike," he replied. He scratched his red hair, frowning. "I've got to stop making bets with you, Alex. You win every bet. I don't know how you do it. I'm totally broke."

"Just a lucky streak," I said, forcing myself not to grin. "Listen, leave your bike. You can get it tomorrow. Come to my house for dinner."

He shook his head. "I can't. It's going to rain. I want to get home fast."

"But—but—"

The final buzzer drowned out my protests.

I can't stop him from riding his bike, I realized. But I *can* stop him from having an accident.

I'll run along beside him. I'll make sure he pays attention and watches where he's going.

I can stop this accident from happening. I *will* stop it!

"Here's your five bucks," a kid grumbled. He shoved a five-dollar bill into my hand. "You're too lucky, Alex."

Two other guys each counted out five singles and handed them over to me. "Hey—double or nothing next time!" I shouted happily.

I collected all my winnings. Then I carefully counted the money to make sure I had it all. "Thirty-eight . . . thirty-nine . . . forty. Yes!"

If I kept winning like this, I'd soon have enough money to buy a new guitar!

I turned to Shawn. "Hey—"

He was gone. I thought he was standing right beside me.

The gym was emptying out slowly. I pushed my way desperately through the crowd and squeezed out the door. Some girls down the hall called to me, but I didn't turn around. I had to find Shawn.

I pushed open the back doors of the school building and burst onto the parking lot. It was a dark, damp evening. Black storm clouds spread over the sky. I felt a few cold drops of rain on my forehead.

"Shawn—?"

I spotted him on his bike, pedaling hard, speeding away from the bike rack.

"Shawn—stop!" I shouted, waving both arms. I took off, running after him.

I saw Tessa at the bike rack with two other girls. She looked up as I ran past. "Alex—what's up?"

I didn't slow down. I chased after Shawn, waving my arms frantically, shouting his name. "Stop! Hey—stop!"

He didn't hear me. He rolled down Park Street, picking up speed.

Rain began to patter down. I tried to run faster, ignoring the ache in my side.

"Shawn! Stop! Hey—Shawn!" I screamed.

Finally, he heard me.

He turned around.

"Stop!" I shouted, cupping my hands around my mouth. "Stop!"

He stared at me. He didn't see the large yellow moving van parked at the curb.

"Noooooo!"

My scream was too late.

His bike smashed into the broad back of the truck. I heard a sick crunch of metal. Then I heard Shawn's shrill cry.

The crash threw him into the air. His hands flew straight up. He smacked the back of the truck. Bounced off. Hit the pavement, landing on his side.

And didn't move.

I stood frozen in the middle of the street, staring in horror, my hands still cupped around my mouth.

My fault, I thought.

Then I heard a voice shouting. A familiar voice.

And I saw Tessa running along the curb, her blond hair flying behind her. She dropped down on the pavement beside Shawn.

"Alex—" she called. "Don't just stand there! Go get help! Get to a phone! Call for help! Hurry!"

Her cries broke through my thoughts. I shook myself alert and started to run up the driveway of the nearest house. They'll let me use the phone, I told myself. I'll call 911.

But as I ran up the drive, the same thought kept repeating in my mind.

My fault.

The accident was my fault. If I hadn't been there, Shawn wouldn't have turned around. If I hadn't been there, he'd be okay right now.

My fault . . .

The diary's fault . . .

I have to get rid of that diary, I decided. I have to get rid of it and never read another entry.

But will that help?

Will the horrible things stop happening to my friends and me?

After dinner, I sat at my desk, staring at the diary. I held it between my hands, rubbing my fingers over the smooth black leather cover. I felt a chill of fear.

I'm not going to read another entry, I vowed.

How many frightening things had happened since I'd found the diary? I ran through them again in my mind. I was hit by a car . . . jumped off the school roof . . . and now Shawn was lying in the hospital with a badly broken leg.

I squeezed the little book tightly. My hands were sweating. They left wet fingerprints on the leather.

Can I really just toss this amazing book away? I asked myself. What about all the bets I've been winning?

The Ravens have four more basketball games to play. If I keep winning, I'll have more than enough for a new guitar. I'll be able to buy that Fender Strat I've been wanting for years!

No. Forget about that, Alex, I told myself. Give up

betting. Give it up before it's too late.

Be smart. Get rid of the diary. Throw it away.

But what if that doesn't help? I asked myself. The question sent a chill down my back.

What makes you think that all these frightening things will end just because you don't read the diary's predictions?

I stared hard at the book. It appeared to glow like a black jewel in my hands.

My hands trembled. I couldn't help myself. I couldn't stop myself. I started to open the cover.

I heard a cough.

I dropped the book and glanced up. "Tessa—?"

She stepped into my room. Her blond hair was brushed straight back, tied with a bright blue Scrunchie. Her green eyes locked on mine.

"What's going on, Alex?" she demanded. She walked up to my desk and crossed her arms in front of her.

"Excuse me? What do you mean?" I slid open the desk drawer and shoved the diary inside.

"I watched you this afternoon," Tessa said. "And I know there's something weird going on."

I crossed my arms too. "The only weird thing going on is you bursting into my room all the time," I said.

"Why did you run after Shawn like that?" she demanded. "Why did you shout like that?"

"Uh . . . well . . ." I couldn't think of a good answer.

"You knew he was going to crash," Tessa said. "That's why you were trying to stop him."

"No way—!" I cried.

"Yes, I watched you," she insisted. "How did you know he was going to crash?"

"I—I didn't," I told her.

Tessa wouldn't stop asking questions. "Why have you been acting so weird, Alex? I heard about you jumping off the roof at school. Why did you do that?"

"It was no big deal," I said.

She stared at me for a long time. "I have an idea," she said finally. "Remember, you wanted to share diaries. You read mine, and I read yours. Well, okay. Let's try it. Let me see your diary and—"

"NO!" I shouted. I jumped up from my desk and turned to block her way to the desk drawer. "Forget it, Tessa. I'm not sharing. I don't know why you came over here to spy on me. But I'm—"

Her expression changed. She looked really hurt. "I'm not *spying* on you, Alex," she whispered. "I'm just . . . worried about you. I mean, now that I'm in your band, I thought . . . I thought maybe we'd be friends."

"Friends?" My voice cracked on the word. "Well . . . I don't know . . ."

Now she looked even more hurt. Her red, heart-shaped lips were pushed forward in a sad pout. She sighed. "When is the band going to rehearse? Uncle Jon says the garage is all ready for us."

I was glad she had decided to change the subject. "Let's see if everyone can get together Friday night," I said.

A few minutes later, she was gone.

I made sure I heard the front door close behind her. Then I pulled the diary from its hiding place in the desk drawer.

"I'm not sharing you with anyone!" I told it.

I knew I shouldn't. But I couldn't help myself. I flipped quickly through the pages. Yes. A new entry, an entry for tomorrow:

DEAR DIARY,

What a wild day! Unbelievable!

When the driver got off the school bus for a few minutes, I took over the wheel. Do you believe it? I drove the bus! I raced it halfway across town.

Kids were crying and screaming. But what a thrill!

That is totally insane! I told myself.

I read the entry again. Then I burst out laughing. Why would I do such a crazy thing?

Take over the school bus and drive it across town?

I would never do anything like that. This time, the diary is completely off. Completely wrong.

Besides, Mom picks me up on Thursdays. I don't even *ride* the school bus tomorrow. So it can't happen. It can't.

"Alex, are you up there?"

I heard Mom's shout from the stairs. "Yes? What is it?" I called.

"I can't pick you up after school tomorrow. I have an appointment. You'll have to take the school bus."

After school the next day, I walked to the back of the school bus and plopped down in the very last seat. I fastened the seat belt as tight as I could. And I gripped the arms of the seat.

I'm not going to get up from this seat, I told myself. No matter what happens.

I'm going to show the diary that *I'm* the boss.

I decide what happens and what doesn't.

But I knew I didn't have much of a chance. I'd said the very same words before—and the diary's prediction always came true.

The diary was always right.

Why should I even try to fight it? I wondered.

I'm going to take over the bus, just as the diary said.

Before the ride is over, I'm going to be sitting behind the wheel, taking this thing through town.

I slumped sadly in the seat. The kid next to me said something, but I didn't even answer him. I stared glumly out the window.

Some kids were batting a balloon back and forth down the bus. I didn't even move when the balloon bounced off my head.

Some kids laughed at me. I didn't care.

You won't be laughing soon, I thought bitterly.

Soon you'll be screaming.

How is it going to happen this time? I wondered. What is going to cause me to run up to the front, drop behind the wheel, and drive this bus away?

I saw Billy Miller climb onto the bus, carrying a stack of comic books. He took a seat near the front and started shuffling through them. Was it going to be Billy's fault again?

What is going to make me do such a crazy thing?

I was so tense, I accidentally bit my tongue. I cried out in pain.

I can't take this suspense! I thought.

Finally, Mr. Fenner, the bus driver, climbed into the bus. He shouted for everyone to sit down. Then he slid into the driver's seat and started the engine.

The bus rumbled and shook. Mr. Fenner gunned the engine, making the bus roar and sending a white cloud of exhaust rising up to the back window.

He started to close the door, then changed his mind. The kids all groaned as he climbed up from his seat and stepped down off the bus.

I watched him cross the street to talk to two men at the corner. The two men laughed about something.

Mr. Fenner took off his cap and scratched his gray hair.

"We want to go! We want to go!" some kids started to chant.

Mr. Fenner kept on chatting with the two men. I think he was pretending he couldn't hear the chant.

Without even realizing it, I had unfastened my seat belt and stepped into the aisle.

Why am I doing this? I asked myself.

But the bus, the kids, the long aisle to the driver's seat, were all a blur. I was moving as if in a dream.

In a daze, I walked up the narrow aisle. Kids were chanting. "We want to go! We want to go!"

Billy Miller called out to me. A girl shouted, "Hey, Alex—sit down!"

But I paid no attention to any of them.

I have no choice, I told myself. Some strange force is pulling me forward . . . pulling me . . .

I slid behind the wheel. I gripped it with both hands.

"Alex—what are you doing?" a girl screamed.

"Go! Go! Go!" some kids were chanting.

I saw Mr. Fenner through the bus windshield. He had his back turned. He was shaking his head and laughing with the two men.

I closed the bus door. The engine hummed loudly. I leaned over the wheel. I pressed my foot down on the brake a couple of times, testing it. Then my foot found the gas pedal.

"Go! Go! Go!"

"Stop him!" someone shouted.

"Alex—get back to your seat!" a boy cried.

"Alex—don't!"

They didn't understand. I *had* to take over the bus. I had no control . . . no control at all.

Some kids were screaming for Mr. Fenner. A little girl right behind me started to cry.

I took a deep breath. Then I spun the wheel away from the curb, pulled back the gearshift, and stepped on the gas.

The bus squealed and lurched forward. "Whoa!" I cried out as the side of the bus scraped the car parked in front of us. I saw the car's mirror rip away.

Kids screamed and shrieked.

"Stop!"

"Somebody stop him!"

I spun the wheel harder and pressed the gas pedal down. "Hey—!" The bus rocked over the other curb onto the grass.

Kids shrieked louder.

Steering this thing was a lot harder than I thought.

Of course, I'd never driven a bus before. I'd never driven *anything* before—except in video games!

I jerked the wheel and aimed the bus back into the street. A car horn blared at my side. "LOOK OUT!" I screamed. The bus swerved sharply—and a kid went flying off his bike.

Close call!

"Stop! Alex—stop!" kids were shrieking and crying.

In the mirror, I saw Mr. Fenner running frantically after the bus. His cap blew off his head, but he kept chasing after me.

I leaned over the wheel and struggled to keep the bus on the street. My foot pressed harder on the gas.

How fast was I going?

I didn't dare take my eyes away from the windshield to check the speedometer.

I roared through a stop sign. My foot missed the brake pedal.

Driving was a *lot* harder than I'd imagined.

Behind me, my passengers had grown very silent. I heard a few kids snuffling, a few sobbing. But the screams had stopped. No one was talking.

The bus bounced hard along the street. On both sides, the lawns were a blur of green. I checked the mirror. I had left Mr. Fenner far behind.

When I heard the siren, my breath caught in my throat. I started to choke.

The high wailing sound grew louder. In the mirror, I saw a black police car, red lights flashing.

The diary didn't say anything about police! I thought.

And then my hands slid off the wheel as the bus lurched onto the grass.

The tree rose up in front of me. So dark and wide.

My scream rang out over the sound of the siren.

And then a thundering crash shook the bus.

The tree appeared to fly into the windshield. And all the sounds meshed together—my scream . . . the siren wail . . . the shattering glass . . . and the crunch of bending metal.

Then silence.

A terrifying, ugly silence.

"Why did you do it, Alex?"

Dad held me by the shoulders. His eyes studied my face.

"I . . . can't explain," I whispered. "I'm . . . really sorry."

Mom and Dad came to the police station to take me home. They were too shocked and confused to be angry at me.

Why *had* I done it?

I really couldn't explain it. And if I told my parents about the diary, they wouldn't believe it anyway.

Luckily, none of the kids on the bus had been hurt. The front of the bus was pretty smashed in. And the tree I hit didn't exactly look great.

"You have no explanation?" Mom asked, biting her bottom lip. "No explanation at all for doing such a stupid, dangerous thing?"

"It won't happen again," I muttered.

And I meant it.

The diary had to go. I wasn't going to keep it for one more night.

Once again, Tessa appeared in my room after dinner. "I know why you're doing these things, Alex," she said, sneering at me. "I know your secret."

Had she really figured it out? I stared at her. "Secret?"

"It's the diary," she said.

I swallowed hard. How did she know? "What about the diary?" I demanded.

She narrowed her green eyes at me. "You're doing all these crazy, dangerous things *just so you'll have something exciting to write in your diary!*" she declared.

I laughed. She didn't have a clue.

"You've pulled all these crazy stunts so that your diary will be more exciting than mine," Tessa continued. "And then you'll win our bet."

She shook her head. "Alex, how could you risk all those kids' lives just to win a bet?"

I tried to explain to her that she was way off. That she didn't know what she was talking about. "I'm finished betting on things," I said. "I'm never going to make another bet as long as I live." But I couldn't convince her.

When she finally left, I grabbed the diary. I held it in my hands, staring at the cover.

I really wanted to read it. I really wanted to see

what it said about tomorrow.

Maybe just a peek . . .

No!

It was too dangerous. I could have killed those kids on the bus this afternoon. I could have killed myself! What if tomorrow's entry was even more dangerous and terrifying?

No. No way. This time I meant it.

Gripping the diary tightly in my hand, I crept out to the backyard. It was a dark night, but the three metal trash cans lined up at the side of the garage were easy to find. I lifted the lid off the first can.

A cold breeze made the trees shiver. A low tree branch cracked—and fell, thudding to the ground behind me.

Startled, I dropped the lid. My heart pounding, I tossed the diary into the can.

When I bent to pick up the lid, I heard a sound. A crackling. A scraping.

Another tree branch shifting in the wind?

Or was someone out there in the darkness, watching me?

"Who's there?" I called. "Is someone there?"

Silence.

Shivering, I made my way back into the house. I was glad to be rid of the diary. I felt a hundred pounds lighter.

That night, I fell asleep quickly. I dreamed I was floating, floating on a puffy white cloud. The cloud suddenly popped and vanished—and I woke up.

I sat straight up, wide awake. Panic choked my throat. I glanced at the clock. Three in the morning.

I don't know what's going to happen tomorrow, I thought. I pictured the diary out back in the trash can.

I need it, I told myself. I need to know what's going to happen. I *have* to know!

I climbed out of bed. I straightened my pajama bottoms and crept barefoot down the stairs.

Once again, I was moving as if in a daze. As if under a spell. I knew I shouldn't be doing this. I knew I should leave the diary in the trash.

But I couldn't help myself. I had to read what it said about tomorrow.

I clicked on the light to the backyard. I silently prayed it wouldn't wake Mom and Dad. Carefully, I unlocked the kitchen door, pulled it open, and slipped out into the cold, moonless night.

Trees creaked and groaned. The wet grass felt icy cold against my bare feet. I saw an animal slither under a bush. I think it was a mole or a raccoon.

I tiptoed to the trash cans. The wind made my pajama shirt ripple. Shivering hard, I lifted the lid off the first can. I bent over it. Reached inside.

"Huh?"

No diary.

I leaned closer. Dipped my head into the can. No diary.

With a low cry, I began pawing frantically through the trash. It *has* to be here! I told myself. It has to!

Bending over the can, searching furiously, I dug deeper, deeper into the trash.

Where is it? Where?

In a panic, I lifted the can in both hands. Turned it upside down. And poured everything out.

Then I dropped to my knees on the wet grass and began tearing through the trash. Grabbing at it. Heaving it aside.

"Where is it?" I cried out loud, my heart thudding in my chest. "It's got to be here!"

I grabbed the next can and tilted it over. Nothing. No sign of the diary.

I turned the third can over too. Gagged on the smell of sour milk. Tore through the trash bags. Tore through spoiled eggs and wilted, decayed lettuce.

Tossed it all away. Tossed it over the lawn. Searching . . . searching in a choking panic.

But no. No diary.

The diary was gone.

I stayed awake the rest of the night. I paced back and forth in my room, thinking about the diary.

It didn't just disappear, I knew. Someone had taken it.

Was it Tessa?

It didn't take me long to find out.

In school the next morning, I felt tense, shaky. One reason was that I'd been awake all night. But mainly, I was tense because I didn't know what was going to happen.

In algebra class, we had a pop quiz. I totally flunked it. I hadn't even opened my algebra book the night before.

As I slunk out of the room, I glimpsed the broad grin on Tessa's face. "That was so easy," she declared.

Later, I saw Tessa in the hall surrounded by a group of her friends. "Is it a bet?" she was saying.

"Let me get this straight," her friend Nella said. "You want to bet us five dollars there will be a gym locker inspection this afternoon?"

Tessa nodded, grinning. "Who wants to bet five bucks?"

"But we *never* have gym locker inspections!" Nella protested.

"If we don't, you win the bet," Tessa said.

I watched as the girls reached into their bags, pulling out five-dollar bills. Why was Tessa so sure about the locker inspection?

There was only one answer to that question. The diary. She knew the future. She must have the diary.

I balled my hands into tight fists. I gritted my teeth, trying not to explode in anger.

At lunchtime, I ran to catch up to her. "Hey, Tessa—wait up! I know what you did—"

"Better hurry, Alex!" she shouted, running ahead of me toward the lunchroom. "Pizza today!"

"How do you know?" I called.

Her green eyes lit up gleefully. "A little birdie told me!" She laughed and trotted into the lunchroom.

Again, I balled my hands into fists. Tessa has it, I knew. She waited till I went inside last night. Then she took the diary.

But she isn't keeping it for long, I decided. I'm going to get it back—tonight.

After dinner, Dad drove Chip and me to Tessa's uncle's house. We carried our guitars into the garage and set them down against the wall. Dad carried the large amp over to the electrical outlet near the door.

"I've got to go, guys," he said. "I'll pick you up in a few hours. Have a good practice."

"Thanks for helping us carry our stuff," Chip called as my dad climbed back into the car.

A few seconds after he backed away, Tessa appeared. She carried a tall stack of papers. "I brought some songs we can try," she said.

"Your uncle's garage is awesome," Chip said. He bent to plug his guitar into the amp. "We've got enough electrical power in here to rehearse an orchestra!"

Tessa nodded. "Uncle Jon is a good guy." She turned to the driveway. "Hey—look who's here!"

We all turned to watch Shawn struggle up the drive on his crutches. He had a heavy white cast on his broken leg that reached all the way to his waist.

Chip hurried to carry Shawn's guitar for him. "Hey, Shawn—how are you going to play guitar with those crutches?" he asked.

Shawn snickered. "I guess maybe I'll put the crutches down when I play," he said.

We all laughed. Chip blushed bright red.

The night was overcast, and a sudden flash of lightning made the garage as bright as day. A soft rain started to fall, tapping against the garage windows and the roof.

Chip attached a cable to Shawn's guitar. "I'll help you set up."

A boom of thunder shook the walls. "Great sound effects!" Chip cried.

I suddenly realized that Tessa was staring at me. "What's your problem, Alex?" she asked. "Why are you just standing around?"

"Oh. Uh . . . I brought the wrong guitar," I said. "I really wanted to play the other one."

I started toward the open garage door. Lightning flickered over the trees across the street. "I'm going to run home and get it," I said, shouting over another burst of thunder.

"In the rain?" Shawn called.

"It's only a couple of blocks," I said. "I'll be back by the time you're set up." I pulled my jacket over my head, grabbed my backpack, and ran out of the garage.

Of course, I wasn't going to my house. I was going to Tessa's house.

I had planned this all afternoon. I was going to Tessa's house to get back my diary.

The rain came down a little harder. My shoes splashed through shallow puddles as I jogged along the sidewalk. Lightning streaked the sky, making the trees and lawns flash like silver.

A few minutes later, I stepped onto Tessa's front stoop. Tessa's mom answered the door. "Alex? What's wrong?" she asked, very shocked to see me. "You're soaked!"

"Tessa forgot some song sheets," I said. "She asked me to get them from her room."

Thunder boomed. Dr. Wayne shook her head. "I hope you kids are all right in this storm. Practicing in a garage . . ."

"It's a very well-built garage," I said. "No leaks or anything."

I wiped my wet shoes carefully on the welcome mat, then made my way to Tessa's room. I clicked on the light—and saw it instantly.

The diary. *My* diary. Lying on top of a stack of papers on Tessa's desk.

"Yessss!" I cried happily.

I dove across the room and grabbed it.

She stole it. Tessa stole my diary! How could she do a thing like that?

Well, it doesn't matter, I decided. The diary is back with its proper owner.

I held it in my hands. Rainwater dripped from my hair onto the leather cover. I brushed the water away with my finger.

I've got to open it, I decided. I've got to see what the diary says about tonight.

I've felt so lost without it . . . so totally lost.

My hands shook as I flipped the book open.

I shuffled past the old entries till I came to the last page.

The new entry. The entry for tonight.

My eyes bulged as I read it. One word.

Only one word on the page:

DEAD.

DEAD.

I stared at the word, the book trembling between my hands.

.My frightening dream flashed into my mind. The dream had come true. The diary entry read: DEAD.

And the diary never lied.

"Alex—did you find what you need?" Dr. Wayne's voice broke into my thoughts.

"Yes. No problem!" I called. I slammed the book shut. I stuffed it into my backpack. Then I headed back to the front of the house.

DEAD.

Whoa. Wait a minute.

Tessa stole the diary yesterday. And now the entry for today was that one frightening word.

It means that Tessa is in danger, I realized. Not me.

I called good night to her mother and ran back into the rain. It was coming down harder now. Sheets of rain lit up by bright flashes of crackling lightning.

I pulled my jacket over my head and ran.

Tessa is in danger. The diary says that Tessa will be dead.

I can't let that happen, I decided. I have to warn her.

Thunder boomed. A jagged bolt of lightning snapped over the grass, so close, I jumped back.

My shoes splashed up waves of water.

DEAD. DEAD.

I'm going to save Tessa, I vowed. I'm going to save her.

But—how?

A car rolled past, windshield wipers snapping. I leaped back as the tires sent up a tidal wave of water.

Through sheets of rain, the garage came into view. I could see my friends beyond the garage window.

My shoes pounded up the driveway. I was only a few feet from the garage when I heard a loud *crack*.

I glanced up in time to see a white bolt of lightning hit the tree beside the garage.

I heard a *snap*—and then a sizzling rip.

A large tree branch shuddered, then fell. It crashed with a wet *thud* to the soaked lawn.

Shaking, I struggled to pull open the garage door. As the door slid up, I saw Tessa. She was bending over to plug in a microphone cord.

Thunder boomed.

Tessa held the microphone in one hand while she struggled to plug in the cord.

She's going to be hit by lightning, I realized.

DEAD.

DEAD.

Tessa is going to be hit by lightning.

That's how the diary prediction will come true—unless I get to her in time.

Lightning streaked low over the garage roof. I heard the loud *crack* as it hit the wooden fence at the back of the yard.

Shaking off water, I lurched into the garage.

"Tessa—drop the cord!" I shrieked.

At the sound of my cry, all three of them turned.

"Drop it!" I shouted. "Tessa—drop it *now*!"

Tessa squinted at me. "Alex? What's your problem?"

She finished plugging in the cord. She held the microphone at her waist.

"Drop it!" I screamed.

And then I dove across the garage, my wet shoes slipping on the concrete floor.

Thunder roared.

I leaped across the garage—and grabbed the microphone from Tessa's hand.

As I grabbed it away, I saw the flash. A blinding white flash. So bright, so white, it forced my eyes shut.

And then I felt the jolt. A bone-crushing jolt of pain.

Like being hit by a locomotive.

The current crackled around me. My teeth chattered. My eyeballs burned.

And then the sizzling . . . the sizzling . . .

The sound of my own skin sizzling, burning away beneath the crackling electricity.

Hit by lightning . . .

Hit by lightning . . .

A roar of thunder was the last sound I heard.

When the thunder faded, I slowly opened my eyes.

I gazed around my room. My own bedroom. I stood in my room.

"Surprise, Alex!" Mom cried.

Two men in blue uniforms were carrying an old desk into my room.

Mom smiled. "Do you like it? This is the desk you've needed for so long."

I gaped at it. "Huh? A desk? Hey—thanks!" I cried.

The phone rang. Mom hurried downstairs to answer it.

After the two men left, I began to examine the desk. It was very cool. Big. Dark wood. Very old-fashioned-looking.

I began opening the drawers. Some of them stuck a little. I had to struggle to pull them open.

"Hey!" I cried out when I found the little book in the bottom drawer. I lifted it out, blew the dust off it, and examined it.

A diary.

How strange, I thought. This morning, Miss Gold suggested that I keep a diary for extra credit. And then Tessa Wayne had wanted to keep a diary too.

And here it is—a diary. A blank diary.

Or *is* it blank?

To my surprise, I saw an entry already written in the book. In *my handwriting*!

But how could that be?

Very confused, I raised the diary close and began to read the entry:

DEAR DIARY,

The diary war has started, and I know I'm going to win. I can't wait to see the look on Tessa's face when she has to hand over one hundred big ones to me.

I ran into Tessa in the hall at school, and I started teasing her about our diaries. I said that she and I should share what we're writing—just for fun. I'll read hers, and she could read mine.

Tessa said no way. She said she doesn't want me stealing her ideas. I said, "Whatever." I was just trying to give her a break and let her see how much better my diary is going to be than hers.

Then I went into geography class, and Mrs. Hoff horrified everyone by giving a surprise test on chapter eight. No one had studied chapter eight. And the test was really hard. . . .

My hands were shaking. My heart was pounding. I stared at the diary in amazement.

That entry is for tomorrow, I realized.

But how does the diary know what will happen tomorrow?

IT'S AS IF IT ALREADY HAPPENED!

I glanced over the entry again.

"It can't be true—*can* it?" I asked myself.

Well . . . Just in case, I decided . . . maybe I'll study chapter eight right now!

ABOUT THE AUTHOR

R.L. STINE says he has a great job. "My job is to give kids the CREEPS!" With his scary books, R.L. has terrified kids all over the world. He has sold over 300 million books, making him the best-selling children's author in history.

These days, R.L. is dishing out new frights in his series THE NIGHTMARE ROOM. When he isn't working, he likes to read old mysteries, watch *SpongeBob Squarepants* on TV, and take his dog, Nadine, for long walks around New York City, where he lives with his wife, Jane, and son, Matthew.

"I love taking my readers to scary places," R.L. says. "Do you know the scariest place of all? It's your MIND!"

Take a look at what's ahead in

THE NIGHTMARE ROOM #6
They Call Me Creature

"CAW CAW CAW CAW!"

"It's okay, Mr. Crow," I said softly. I finished bandaging the bird and set it down gently in its cage.

"CAWW CAWWW!" It struggled to flutter its broken wing.

Dad slammed the magazine he was reading down on the table. He squinted at me through his thick, black-framed glasses. "Laura, could you shut that bird up?"

I caught the surprise on my friend Ellen's face. She hadn't seen Dad's new grouchy personality.

Lucky, the big stray dog I found in the woods, bumped past me, nearly knocking over the birdcage. He began licking Dad's hand with his fat tongue.

Dad jerked the hand away. "Would you get this slobbering mutt out of here?" he snapped. "Yuck. What a disgusting animal."

"You're a vet!" I cried. "You're supposed to love animals—remember?" I sighed. "Besides, where am I supposed to put him? I can't use the shed anymore since you're working in there."

Dad rolled his eyes. "Why can't I live in a house,

Laura? Why do I have to live in a stinking zoo?"

Ellen forced a laugh. But I could see she was really embarrassed. She had never seen Dad and me yelling at each other. She hadn't seen Dad since . . . since he changed.

"CAW CAWWWW." The crow hopped up and down, uttering its shrill cries.

I picked up the cage and grabbed Lucky by the collar. I took them both down the hall to my room and shut the door.

I swung my camera around my neck. "Come on, Ellen," I said. "Let's get to the woods."

That's where I feel the happiest. It's so beautiful in the woods, so peaceful and filled with life.

Our back lawn ends at the woods. So I've always considered the miles and miles of trees and little streams part of my backyard.

I checked out my camera, making sure I had put in a fresh film cartridge.

Ellen brushed back her straight, black hair. She loves her hair. She's always pushing it back, pulling it to the side, sweeping her hands through it.

I'm totally jealous of her hair. Mine is short, and red-brown, and frizzy.

Ellen's eyes flashed. "Are we going into the woods because of your science project? Or because you want to find that boy you met?"

I let out a groan. "Because of my project," I said. "Life isn't only about boys, you know."

She laughed. "Says who?"

"Some people have other interests," I sneered. I didn't want to admit that I'd been thinking about Joe a lot since I ran into him by Luker Pond.

"Let's get out of here," I said. "We just have to find Georgie." I started to the back door.

"You're going into the woods?" Dad asked, frowning at me. "Don't bring back any more strays. I mean it."

"Okay, okay," I muttered.

I sighed. In the past few weeks, Dad had changed completely. He had loved animals his whole life. That's where I got it from. But now he complained about every stray I found.

Since I was a little girl, he and I always roamed the woods for hours and hours, exploring, talking, laughing. We could always talk about *anything*.

Now he spent all of his time locked up in the little shed in our backyard. And he had become silent and grouchy. Sometimes he didn't even answer when I spoke to him.

I tried to tell Mom about it during one of our long phone talks. But we had a bad connection, and I don't think she understood.

Mom moved to Chicago after she and Dad divorced. Sometimes I really miss talking with her. Phone calls and e-mail just aren't the same.

I see her a lot. But my parents gave me a choice, and I chose to live with Dad. I just don't like big cities. I have to be near the woods.

Shaking my head, I followed Ellen to the back door.

She's tall and skinny and all legs, like a deer. With her big, dark eyes and sort-of innocent, round face, Ellen reminds me of a delicate, graceful doe.

If she's a doe, I'm a fox. My red-brown hair is kind of like fox fur. I'm short and quick, and I have wide-apart brown eyes and a foxy smile.

I'm always comparing all the kids I know to animals. I guess it's because I love animals so much.

Ellen and I stepped out into a cool, crisp spring day. A string of puffy clouds floated low over the trees. The air smelled fresh and sweet.

"Sorry about Dad," I said to Ellen. "He's been such a sourpuss ever since he left his job at the animal hospital."

Ellen shrugged. Her eyes were on the sky.

I heard a flapping noise from the woods. It sounded like hundreds of hands clapping.

The sky darkened very suddenly. As if someone had clicked off all the lights.

I blinked, startled. And turned to the woods.

"Huh? What on earth!" I cried. I thought I was watching a black tornado swirling, spinning above the trees.

Ellen grabbed my arm. "Wow. What *is* that?" she whispered.

"Birds!" I gasped. "I've—I've never seen birds that swarm like that!"

Hundreds of birds flew in a tight circle, like a black funnel cloud, screeching and cawing. The squawking birds flew round and round, rising in the sky until they blocked the sunlight.

A shadow fell over me.

I turned and saw that Dad had followed us outside. Behind his thick glasses, he gazed up at the sky. He shuddered. I caught his expression of fear.

"Something has them stirred up," he said. "Something is wrong out there, Laura. Don't go. Don't go into the woods today."

"I—I have to go," I replied. "My project . . ."

Dad stared at the swirling black funnel cloud of shrieking birds. "Birds don't act like that unless something is terribly wrong," he said softly.

And then he took off, running full speed across the back lawn.

"Dad!" I shouted. "Dad—where are you going? Come back!"

He didn't turn around. I watched him vanish into the trees.

"What is he doing?" Ellen asked, her hands pressed to her face. "He's running right into it!"

We stood there, huddled together. We watched the dark cloud of birds, circling, circling, the shrill, frantic cries echoing off the trees.

Then the cries stopped. The roar of flapping wings faded. The birds swooped down, down to the trees. The sky glowed in the sunlight again. And once again, I could hear the gentle rush of the wind.

It was all over in less than a minute. But what a strange and frightening minute.

"Dad?" I called, cupping my hands around my mouth. "Dad? Where are you?"

No reply.

I had felt uncomfortable, edgy, all day, I realized. Maybe it's because I'm so in tune with the woods.

When I'm in the woods, I can always sense when there's danger nearby. I always get a tingling feeling when there's some kind of trouble around.

"Looks like the coast is clear," Ellen said, brushing her hair back. She took a few steps towards the trees. "Maybe we'll catch up with your dad in there."

"Maybe," I said. I heard the soft thud of footsteps. Georgie, my German shepherd, came trotting around the side of the house. His tail started wagging when he saw us.

He came running up to me first. He knows I'm his best friend. I grabbed his neck, and we started wrestling on the grass.

"We're bringing Georgie with us—right?" Ellen asked.

I nodded. "Of course. I wouldn't go into the woods without him. Georgie and I have been exploring the woods together since he was a little puppy."

Ellen led the way, and I followed after her. The camera bounced against my chest as I walked. "My project is due in less than two weeks," I groaned.

"And I hardly have any photos."

My science project was to study the animal life at Luker Pond. The idea was to photograph the pond every day for three weeks and see how many different kinds of animals I could find that use the pond.

I thought it would be easy. But I had been at the pond every afternoon for a week, and I was having trouble finding animals.

Ellen jogged across the grass. Her hair swung behind her like a horse's tail. Georgie and I caught up with her at the edge of the woods.

She still had her eyes on the sky above the trees. "That was so totally weird," she muttered. "Do you think some big animal frightened the birds from their nests?"

"I don't know," I replied. "And why did my dad—"

I stopped short when I heard the howl.

A high, shrill cry. The sound of an animal in pain.

Georgie raised his head, tensed his back, and started to bark furiously.

The animal howled again.

I spun around. "Whoa. It's coming from the garden shed," I said, pointing.

The shed is square and wood-shingled. It stands halfway between the house and the woods. It's nearly as big as a one-car garage, with a solid wood door and a flat roof.

"What's in there?" Ellen asked. "What poor creature could be crying like that?"

"I don't know," I told her. "Dad has been using the shed for his work. He won't let me go near it."

Ellen squinted hard at the shed. The howling finally stopped. "What kind of work is he doing in there?"

I sighed. "Something too mysterious to tell me about. I tried to go in and take a look last week. But he keeps it locked."

I leaned down and petted Georgie. "I wish I knew what he's doing in there," I said.

We stepped into the shade of the trees. A winding dirt path curved through tall reeds and a tangle of scrawny shrubs.

"Why did your dad leave his job at the animal hospital?" Ellen asked. "Was he fired?"

"I don't know," I said, pushing a low branch out of the way. "He won't tell me. He's been so quiet. He hardly speaks to me. I think he's really messed up. He's just so . . . sad and angry. He seems totally crushed."

Ellen's eyes flashed. She grabbed my arm. "I know what happened, Laura." A sly grin spread over her face. "I know why he left. Your dad and Dr. Carpenter were going out together—and she dumped him!"

"YUCK!" I exclaimed. I put my finger down my throat and pretended to puke. "That is *so* not what happened," I said. "Dad and Dr. Carpenter? No way."

I've known Dr. Carpenter ever since she moved

here to run the animal hospital four years ago. She's really nice. If she and Dad had some kind of romance going on, I'd know about it.

So why *did* Dad leave? It was a total mystery. Dr. Carpenter always said Dad was the best vet in the world. She wouldn't fire him—would she?

Did he mess up somehow? Did he do something wrong?

I didn't want to think about it.

We climbed over a fallen tree, blanketed with thick green and yellow fungus. We were almost to the pond.

"Let's talk about this fabulous birthday party I'm throwing for you," I said. I wanted to change the subject. "I need a list. Who do you want me to invite?"

"Only boys." Ellen grinned.

"You're joking, right?" I said.

"Why don't you invite that guy you met? Joe," Ellen suggested. "I'd really like to meet him."

"Hey—" I said sharply. "I saw him first!"

I turned and spotted Georgie examining a pile of dead leaves. Sniffing hard, he started to paw furiously at the leaf pile.

"Georgie—get away from there!" I shouted. "Georgie—no!"

Ellen made a disgusted face. "Whoa. What is he doing?"

Ellen doesn't really like being outdoors that much. She'd much rather be home, checking out a stack of fashion magazines, or talking on the phone to guys.

But she's such a good friend, she tags along to keep me company.

"Georgie—get away from there!" I shouted.

The dog ignored me. Grunting, he buried his head in the pile of fat, brown leaves—and pulled out something in his teeth.

"What *is* that?" Ellen cried. She pressed her hands to the sides of her face. "What has he got?"

"Let me see it, Georgie," I said, stepping towards him, reaching out my hand. "Drop. Drop it, boy. What have you got?"

I edged closer. "What is it, boy? What do you have there?"

The dog let out a grunt. Then his jaw snapped open and the object dropped to the ground.

Ellen and I stared down at it—and we both began to scream.

"It—it's a finger!" I cried. "A human finger!"

Georgie barked at it, his tail wagging furiously.

"Oh, gross," Ellen moaned, shutting her eyes. "Is it really a finger? I'm going to be totally sick."

I stepped up to it and poked it with my shoe. I squatted down to see it better.

"Yes, it's a finger," I said weakly. My stomach lurched. I studied it. "But maybe . . . maybe it's not from a person," I told Ellen.

She had her hands over her face and she had

turned away. "Wh-what do you mean?"

"Well . . . the skin is kind of leathery. And the fingernail is pointed. And it's so hairy. . . ."

"SHUT UP!" Ellen screamed. "Don't talk about it anymore! Let's just get away from it." She started back to the path. "Why did your dumb dog pick it up, anyway?"

"Georgie is an explorer, like me," I said. I petted the top of the dog's head and started to follow Ellen. "Looks like it was torn off by another animal. I wonder what kind of animal is strong enough to rip a finger off like that," I said.

"Just shut up about it," Ellen said. "I feel sick. Really."

"Here. Catch!" I shouted.

I pretended to toss it to her.

She screamed and ducked. "Not funny, Laura," she muttered. "Hey—why don't you take a photo of it? For your science project."

"I'm supposed to photograph whole animals," I said. "Not just parts."

White moths fluttered over Luker Pond. High in a tree, I heard the *knock-knock-knock* of a woodpecker. Yes! Excellent! I *needed* that woodpecker! I raised the camera to my eye and searched the tree for it.

"I think I've got to go," Ellen said. "What time is it, anyway?"

I studied the trees through the camera viewfinder. "It's probably close to three."

"Oh, wow. I've *really* got to go," Ellen said. "I promised Stevie Palmer I'd play tennis with him at three." She jumped over a flat stone and started to jog away.

"Excuse me? Stevie Palmer?" I cried. "That *animal?*"

"Don't call him that," Ellen snapped. "He's changed. Really."

How could Ellen be interested in Stevie? No one liked him. Everyone at school laughed at him because of the way he ate. He devoured his food, shoving whole sandwiches into his mouth. He chewed up chicken bones and swallowed them!

Once I saw him shove four Twinkies in his mouth at once! When he left the lunchroom, his table and the floor were covered with food.

Also, Stevie had a terrible temper. He was always getting into fights. Once in fifth grade, he *bit* a girl. And she had to go to the hospital because she got a really bad infection. The rumor was that Stevie had to see a psychiatrist for months after that.

And *he* was Ellen's latest crush?

"I know what you're thinking," Ellen said. "But it's so not fair. Stevie is a great guy now. Invite him to my party. You'll see." She took off again.

"No, wait—" I cried, lowering the camera. "Who else should I invite? Who else?"

She turned back, pulling her hair behind her shoulder. "Invite *everybody!*" she shouted. Then she disappeared behind a clump of evergreen shrubs.

Oh, sure, I thought. I'll invite all twenty of your boyfriends. Then I'll just sit by myself in a corner and watch you flirt with them all. Whoop-de-do.

"Whoa. Bitter. Bitter," I scolded myself.

Why was I suddenly in such a bad mood?

It wasn't just the disgusting finger Georgie found. I'd felt strange all day. As if something was wrong, something I couldn't quite figure out.

I'll feel better once I take some photographs, I decided. I had taken only three or four photos. I desperately needed to find some animals—or my project was going to be a complete failure.

I stepped up to the edge of the pond. Come on, animals. Where are you hiding?

I was so desperate, I snapped a picture of the white moths fluttering above the water.

I'll sit down and wait, I decided. Maybe if I'm really still, some deer will come to drink.

I sat down. And waited. I held my camera in my lap and listened to the whisper of the trees. One of my favorite sounds.

A minute later, I heard another sound—the snap of a twig.

Behind me?

I turned back but didn't see anything.

I stood up. And heard the heavy scrape of hooves.

Was it a deer?

The sounds stopped.

I took three or four steps forward.

Behind me, I heard the footsteps again.

I stopped. And once more, the footsteps stopped.

I shuddered as a tingle of fear ran down my back.

I'm never frightened in the woods. Never. Even when I'm by myself.

But today was different.

The circling birds . . . my dad's warning to stay away . . . the ugly finger in the grass . . .

And now, something was trailing me. Something was creeping up behind me.

"Dad?" I called.

No answer.

I listened hard. Silence now. The excited chitter of birds in a high tree limb. The whisper of wind. The creak of a branch.

Holding my breath, I took another step. Another.

I stopped when I saw the finger in the grass where I left it. I picked it up. I don't know why. I guess I wasn't thinking clearly.

I was listening for the footsteps. And I heard them. The snap of a twig behind me. The heavy thud of shoes or hooves.

With a gasp, I spun around quickly.

"Wh-who's there?" I cried.

A boy stepped out from the trees. He gazed at me shyly, then lowered his dark eyes. He was short and kind of chubby. He had long, black tangles of hair, very shiny, nearly as long as Ellen's.

"Joe—hi!" I called. I breathed a sigh of relief.

"Hey, it's you!" he said, trotting up to me.

I smiled at him. "I heard something following me. I—I didn't know what to think."

Pink circles appeared on his cheeks. "It's only me," he said softly.

He's so totally shy, I realized. And really cute.

He wore baggy denim cutoffs and a black T-shirt. A long silver chain dangled around his neck.

He pointed to my camera. "Snap anything today?"

"No. I . . ." I glanced down and suddenly realized I was holding the disgusting finger. Why had I picked it up? If Joe sees it, he'll think I'm totally weird, I decided.

"I heard a woodpecker in that tree over there," I said, pointing.

When Joe turned to the tree, I let the finger fall from my hand. He turned back—and I stamped my shoe down over it to hide it.

"I'm desperate," I said. "Where are the animals? Are they all on strike?"

"Maybe we could drag some over," Joe said. "You know. Go to a pet store or something. Get some hamsters or turtles and bring them to the pond."

"I don't think so," I said, laughing. "But keep thinking. That was an interesting idea."

We stepped up to the pond. Joe kicked a stone

into the water. His long hair fluttered in the wind.

"How are things at Wilberne Academy?" I asked. I admit it. I had a little bit of a sneer on my face.

He turned to me. "You're making fun of me because I go to a private school, aren't you!"

"No way!" I insisted. "It's just . . . well . . . The guys I know from Wilberne are such snobs. And you don't seem like that."

He snickered. "Hey, thanks. I think."

I decided I'd invite Joe to Ellen's birthday party. The idea made my heart start pounding. I realized I was nervous.

Go ahead, Laura. Just invite him, I told myself. Don't make a big deal about it. Be bold—like Ellen.

I took a deep breath. "Uh . . . Joe?"

Two chattering birds interrupted. They were so loud, right above our heads. I turned in time to see them take off, chirping together as they flew.

Joe and I watched them soar straight up above the treetops. They were joined by three or four other chattering birds. What a racket! They formed a ragged V and flew out of sight.

Joe shook his head. "What's *their* problem?"

We laughed together. I liked the way Joe's eyes narrowed into little moon slivers when he laughed. He reminded me of a bear—a little, friendly bear like the ones you see in cartoons.

I decided to try again. "Uh . . . I'm giving a party for my friend . . ." I started.

I didn't have a chance to finish.

Everything seemed to explode all at once. Trees shook. Animals cried out. Birds cawed and squawked.

The sky blackened as birds took off, flapping their wings wildly. The grass bent as field mice stampeded past our feet.

"Wh-what's happening?" I cried.

Joe spun around, his eyes wide with fright and confusion.

The sky grew even blacker, as if night had fallen.

A shrill, chittering squeal rang out, echoing off the trees. And over the whistlelike cries came the furious flapping of wings.

"Bats!" Joe cried.

Yes. He was right. Bats—hundreds of bats—swarmed above us, squealing, swooping high, then darting into the trees.

"But—but—" I sputtered. "Bats don't fly in the daylight!"

I gasped as a bat swooped over my head. I felt its dry, sharp wing scrape against my face, felt a blast of hot wind off its body.

"Get down, Laura!" Joe grabbed me by the shoulders and pushed me to the ground.

"Cover your head! They're ATTACKING!"